LADY OF

DEVICES

A steampunk adventure novel
Magnificent Devices Book One

Shelley Adina

Moonshell
Books

Moonshell Books
PO Box 752
Redwood Estates, CA 95044
www.shelleyadina.com

Publisher's Note: This is a work of fiction. Names, characters, places, and incidents are a product of the author's imagination. Locales and public names are sometimes used for atmospheric purposes. Any resemblance to actual people, living or dead, or to businesses, companies, events, institutions, or locales is completely coincidental.

Book Layout ©2013 BookDesignTemplates.com
Art by Claudia McKinney at phatpuppyart.com
Design by Kalen O'Donnell at art.kalenodonnell.com
Author font by Anthony Piraino at OneButtonMouse.com

Lady of Devices / Shelley Adina — 2nd ed.
ISBN 978-1-463549-99-2

For Timons Esaias
with special thanks to Spencer Bates

*Thank you to my writers' group: Jasmine
Haynes, Bella Andre, Jenny Andersen, and
Jackie Yau. Without your support and
encouragement, the Lady probably would have
stayed at home.*

London, June 1889

To say the explosion rocked the laboratory at St. Cecelia's Academy for Young Ladies might have overstated the case, but she was still never going to hear the end of it.

Claire Trevelyan closed her eyes as a gobbet of reddish-brown foam dripped off the ceiling and landed squarely on the crown of her head. It dribbled past her ears and onto the pristine sailor collar of her middy blouse, and thence, gravity having its inevitable effect, down the blue seersucker of her uniform's skirt to the floor.

Shrieking, the other students in the senior Chemistry of the Home class had already flung themselves toward the back of the room and away from the benches directly under the mess. "Ladies!" Professor Grünwald shouted, raising his arms as if to calm the stormy waters, "there is no cause for alarm. Collect yourselves, please." His gimlet eyes behind their gleaming spectacles pinned Claire in place like a butterfly on a board. "Miss Trevelyan. Did I not, just moments ago, tell you not to add the contents of that dish to your flask?"

"Yes, sir." She could barely hear herself over the squawking of her classmates.

"Then why did you do it?"

The truth would only net her another grim punishment, but there was no other answer. "To see what would happen, sir."

"Indeed. I seem to remember you gave Doctor Prescott the same reply after the unfortunate incident with the Tesla coil." His jaw firmed under its layer of fat. He addressed the back of the room, where the others huddled against the cabinets in which he kept ingredients and equipment. "Ladies, please. Adding peppermint to an infusion of dandelion and burdock will do you no harm. You may adjourn to the powder rooms to rearrange your toilettes if you must."

Several of the girls stampeded from the room, leaving behind Lady Julia Wellesley, Lady Catherine Montrose, and Miss Gloria Meriwether-Astor, who watched her humiliation with as much wide-eyed delight as if it were the latest flicker at the theater. Claire straightened her spine. She should be used to this. Fortitude was the key.

Another gob of foam landed on her shoulder. Behind her, Lady Catherine stifled a giggle.

"And are you satisfied with your newfound knowledge?" Professor Grünwald was not finished with her yet.

"Yes, sir," Claire said with complete truth.

"I am delighted to hear it. In future, when I tell you not to do something, I would like the courtesy of obedience. You are here to learn the chemistry of the home, not to engage in silly parlor tricks."

"But sir, it would be helpful if you had told us why the compounds should not be mixed."

In the ensuing moment of silence, she heard an indrawn breath of anticipation from the gallery.

"I am sorry to have incommoded you in your quest for information." His sarcasm dripped as unpleasantly as the substance now forming a sticky mass on her clothes. "By tomorrow morning, you will provide me with one hundred lines stating the following: 'I will obey instruction and curb my unladylike curiosity.' Repeat that, please."

Claire did so in a monotone as faithful as any wax recording.

"Thank you, Miss Trevelyan. You will now go and inform the cleaning staff that their assistance is required here."

"Yes, sir."

"And you will stay for the remainder of the period and help them."

Claire clamped her molars down on the urge to further defend herself. "Yes, sir."

"Ladies, class is dismissed. Thank you for your patience."

Patience? He was thanking them? Claire kept her face calm above the storm in her heart as she turned toward the door, the heel of her boot slipping several inches in the foam. Lady Catherine giggled again—Claire suspected she couldn't help herself, being the nervous sort—and the other girls followed her out, careful to keep their clean skirts from touching hers.

"Nicely done, Trevelyan," Lady Julia Wellesley whispered. "We have a half period free thanks to you."

"I must say, that brown substance suits you." Lady Catherine's overbite became more prominent as she smiled. "It's the exact color of your hair."

"Next time, perhaps you'll be less inclined to show off your superior intellectual powers," Gloria Meriwether-Astor added, her flat vowels emphasizing a colonial drawl.

Claire tried to keep silent, but this was just too much. She turned to glare at the new heiress from the American Territories, who had fit in with the other girls from the moment of her arrival like an imperious hand in a kid glove. "I don't show off at all. I—"

"Oh, please," Lady Julia waved her fingers. "Spare us the false humility. But tell me, how on earth do you expect to attract a husband looking like that?"

"She's trying to impress old Grünwald." Lady Catherine giggled. "He's single."

He was also forty if he was a day, overweight, and his receding hairline perspired when he was under pressure, which was nearly all the time. Besides which, marrying anyone below the rank of baron was out of the question, never mind a man forced to earn his living by teaching the next generation of society's glittering lights.

Not that these particular glittering lights wanted to be taught anything but how to embroider a handkerchief or pour a cup of tea. Though if there were a class devoted to the art of landing a titled husband, she had no doubt every one of them would sign up for it and never miss a moment. Of course, Lady Julia could probably teach such a class. Rumor had it that as soon as she descended the platform on graduation day next week, Lord Robert Mount-Batting would go down upon one knee on the lawn and propose. Claire rather doubted that rumor had its facts in order. Lady Julia would never miss her presentation at court in two weeks, nor any of the balls and parties to be held in her honor afterward. If there were to be lawns involved, it would probably be the one at Ascot, or the one at Wellesley House, sometime before the shooting season began in August.

Julia, Catherine, and Claire herself were to be presented to Her Majesty during the same Drawing Room. Claire's imagination shuddered and refused to venture there. Who knew what fresh humiliation those girls could dream up in that most august company?

Finally ridding herself of the maddening crowd, Claire went to Administration and sent a tube contain-

ing Professor Grünwald's request down to the offices of
the staff. No point in cleaning herself up or changing
her clothes if she was to be doomed to pushing a mop
for the next thirty minutes. This benighted school
hadn't the wit to obtain the services of a mother's
helper to take care of the worst of the mess. Armed
with a ladder, mops, and buckets, it took her and the
two chars the rest of the period to clean the sticky foam
off the ceiling, benches, chairs, and floor of the laboratory.

Thank goodness the professor had retired to his office. She was able to laugh at the chars' comments on
his marital prospects with impunity.

After Claire helped them carry the equipment back
to the basement, she changed into her spare uniform in
the gymnasium dressing room as fast as she could. Still,
she arrived at her French class late with half her
blouse's hem sticking out of the waistband of her skirt,
much to the amusement of Lady Julia and Gloria.

"Never mind them," Emilie Fragonard whispered
from the desk behind her as she reached forward and
tucked in the offending article. "You're all right now."

Dear Emilie. Though her friend's hair was drawn
back in an practical braided bun instead of a flattering
pompadour, and her spectacles were, in Claire's opinion, too heavy for her delicate features and hid her fine
eyes, she was the soul of kindness. And kindness,
heaven knew, was in short supply at St. Cecelia's.

After class and before the midday meal, Claire and
Emilie took refuge in the dappled shade under a grove
of trees on the far side of the lawn. Over the ten-foot

granite wall that separated the sheltered young ladies from the bustle of London, the rattle of carriages and jingle of harness could be heard on the road, along with the voices of passers-by and the occasional distinctive chug of a new steam landau. When she heard that sound, Claire could hardly contain the urge to run to the gates and stare. They were such fascinating engines, each one different, yet operating under the same marvelous principles.

"Don't even think about it." Emilie's tone told Claire she'd been caught. "Ladies do not gawk after steam landaus or those who drive them."

"I don't care about who drives them. I drive one myself. I just like to look at them."

"You do not. Drive one, I mean."

"I do indeed. Gorse is teaching me."

"Claire Elizabeth Trevelyan!" Emilie put a pale hand against the trunk of the largest of the elms for support. "I thought your escapade with the quadricycle was bad enough. You cannot tell me you are actually piloting one of those dangerous things!"

"They're not dangerous, if you know their proper operation. Which I do. One's speed and direction are merely a matter of the correct application of steam. The explosions of the first models are a thing of the past."

"That's lucky, knowing how you are about explosions."

Claire's good spirits cooled like a fire left too long without fuel. "You heard."

"The entire school heard. Honestly, dear heart, you've got to curb this unhealthy tendency to blow things up."

"That ridiculous excuse for a professor wouldn't tell us what would happen. How can I be blamed for the silly man's stubbornness? If there's anything I hate, it's someone telling me 'don't' without saying why."

"And one must know the reason why for everything."

"Not everything. But certainly something as simple as why one cannot add a peppermint to dandelion and burdock. One adds peppermint to cookie batter and tea with no harmful effects whatsoever."

"Thanks to you, everyone in school now knows why. And by breakfast tomorrow, everyone at Heathbourne will, too."

Heathbourne was the equivalent of St. Cecelia's on the other side of the square—and where she would have gone had she been born a boy and her father's heir. "I don't care about the opinions of schoolboys."

"You will in a few weeks, when you're at your come-out ball at Carrick House and none of them ask you to dance."

"You sound exactly like my mother." Why had no one told her the bow on the front of her middy blouse was lopsided? She pulled it out and began to retie it.

"In this she's correct, and you know it. Claire, please consider." Emilie's tone became gentle. "It's a fact universally acknowledged that a young lady of good fortune must make a suitable marriage."

"Do not quote the mores of our grandmothers' generation to me. Besides, not every young lady wishes that." Her own appearance taken care of, she reached over to anchor a celluloid hairpin more securely in Emilie's bun. If it could not be lovely, at least it should be secure.

"Every one who wishes to be received in good society does. You don't want to be one of those dreadful Chelsea people, like poor Peony Churchill, do you?"

As a matter of fact, Claire coveted and envied the intellectual explorations found in the salons and lecture halls of the Chelsea set, known in the papers as the Wits. It was led by Mrs. Stanley Churchill, Peony's mother, and populated by explorers and scientists from the Royal Society of Engineers as well as artists, musicians, and the most independent thinkers of Her Majesty Queen Victoria's empire. Their philosophy that the intellect trumped the bloodline flew in the face of most of society. But no one could argue that the Prime Minister himself was one of them. The fact that a scientist or explorer could be granted lands and a title when noble bloodlines were getting more inbred and in some cases dying out altogether was an indication which way the wind blew.

And Claire had always loved the wind. Was it mere coincidence that the family estate in Cornwall was called Gwynn Place, from the Cornish *plas-an-gwyn*, meaning manor of the wind? Perhaps not. Perhaps it was a sign.

A shadow blotted out the sun and she and Emilie looked up to see not a cloud, but an enormous airship passing far overhead. The eleven-thirty packet to Paris had left its mooring mast at Hampstead Heath exactly on time.

Deep in the marble and sandstone halls of the school, a bell rang. "There's lunch," she told Emilie, turning from the wonderful sight of the ship and neatly evading the answer to her friend's question. "Come along or we'll be late."

2

As was his habit, Gorse piloted the steam landau up to the steps in the mews behind St. Cecelia's at precisely three-fifteen. Claire ran to meet him and waited impatiently while he set the brake and went around the front to pull open the thin brass door for her. She allowed him to hand her inside and, with a practiced eye, checked the pressure gauges, the switch positions, and the indicators that told the pilot the levels of coal and water in the boiler.

A hopelessly old-fashioned carriage with the Wellesley family crest on the door rolled up behind them, pulled by two fine chestnuts. Claire could practically feel the stares of envy as Lady Julia and her friends were handed inside.

"Gorse, please, may I—"

"No, miss. The Viscount would have my head were I to allow you to drive this beast in front of those ladies."

What a triumph it would be! "But Gorse—"

"Miss, do not press me, I beg you."

Only consideration for his feelings kept her silent until they were around the corner and halfway down an alley more suited to the collection of trash than the driving of the latest in engines. "Now may I, Gorse?"

"Yes, miss. Remember what I told you about releasing the brake. She'll leap ahead because she's been parked and had a chance to build a bit of a head up."

Claire stepped out without assistance and collected her canvas driving coat from under the folding seat in the rear. Dear Gorse. He insisted on referring to the landau as *she*, as though it were an elegantly built horse made of brass, iron, and glass. But then, people referred to airships as *she*, did they not? The steam landau did have a mind of her own, like a woman of independent thought, that was certain.

She settled into the driving seat as he climbed in on her left. "Gorse, it's a lovely day. We must have the top down."

"Of course, miss."

She braced both feet on the floor and grasped the lever on the side of her seat. As she leaned her weight on it and drew it back, the articulated top of the landau ratcheted back with the whispering sound of a train pulling into a station. It folded itself into a slot behind them like a golden metal fan, and she and Gorse let the glass windows down.

Ahhhhh. Freedom and the wind in her face.

"Mind what I said about the brake, miss. And don't forget these." He handed her a set of driving goggles with a tilt-down telescopic lens to see at greater distance should she need to.

"I remember." It was the work of a moment to remove her broad-brimmed hat and slip the goggles over her eyes to protect them not only from the fug of London's coal fires, but from the very wind of their going. Hat once more in place, she released the brake and the needles on the gauges jumped. Working the brake and the acceleration pedals simultaneously, she controlled the landau's urge to surge ahead until it worked off its head of steam, bowling smartly down the alley and using the horizontal steering lever to turn the corner onto Curzon Street as smoothly as if she hadn't learned to make turns just two weeks ago.

"Well done, miss. Mind that covered conveyance, there. He's stopping."

"I see him." She steered around the enormous lorry filled with lengths of wood for the hotel being constructed on the corner. A cacophony of sound rose around her, from the hammers of the carpenters to the shouts of drivers warning off other people's horses, to the ting of a bell on a shop door opening as they passed.

Their progress slowed to the point that a gaggle of ragamuffins was able to surround the landau and jog alongside it. "Please, miss, have you a halfpenny to spare? Please, miss, we're hungry."

Gorse's jaw set. "Shove off, you lot," he snapped. "Get your grubby paws off this engine!"

To her horror, Claire saw that two of the filthy children were girls of not more than ten. Had they parents? Anyone to look after them? She applied the brake and the landau slowed even further. Digging in the bottom of her school bag, she located a few pence and tossed them to the girls. With shrieks of delight, the little crowd vanished into the warren of alleys behind the construction site.

"Begging your pardon, miss, but you should not encourage beggars." Gorse gazed in the direction they had taken. "It only encourages them to steal from you."

"I gave those pennies voluntarily." She applied steam to the accelerator and they resumed their pace. "And they did look very thin."

Gorse was far too polite to argue with her, even if he was probably right. Didn't the Good Book say that if a person gave a cup of cold water to someone in need, it was the same as giving it to our Lord? She wanted for nothing ... well, nothing of a material kind, at least. Those pennies rolling around in the bottom of her bag would make themselves useful in filling a hungry stomach.

Claire kept a wary eye on the broad avenue in front of her. Large intersections such as the one at Park Lane still intimidated her just a trifle, but with Gorse's patient coaching, they had become easier, especially as she learned to look for spooked horses and impatient young men coming in the other direction. She collected hoots and greetings from one or two of these, but as long as they weren't swearing at her for cutting them off, she was content to blissfully ignore their shouts for her attention.

Not many women knew how to pilot an engine, much less one as pretty as her father's.

And not only pilot it, but suss out the secrets of its operation. Every Saturday morning while the household slept, she and Gorse would examine the inner workings under the landau's gleaming covers. She learned how to fill the coal hopper and top up the boiler. How to clean out the piping and grease the hard-working pistons. She even learned how to balance the delicate platforms that took the weight of coal and water and informed the gauges how much each contained.

Gorse, being a man of intellect and inner resources, knew as much about the physics of steam as any professor at St. Cecelia's. "My grandmother's first cousin on her father's side was Richard Trevithick, the great Cornish engineer," he'd told her one day at the beginning of their secret association. "Engineering runs in our family, you might say. I'd rather tinker with this fine piece of work than run one of his lordship's tin mines, and that's a fact."

Claire deeply regretted the inanity of St. Cecelia's curriculum, which dictated that young ladies should learn dancing, deportment, languages, and the chemistry of the kitchen and cookery rather than practical things like engineering and the operation of steam engines. Who cared how the cake rose? It would do so despite your knowledge of its chemistry, as long as you put the right ingredients into it and applied the right amount of heat. Getting oneself around the country under one's own power—flying upon the ground at the speed of the wind itself—now, that was something worth teaching.

But of course her opinion signified nothing, at school or at home.

A block from Wilton Crescent, the elegant street in Belgravia where Carrick House was situated, she piloted the landau to a grassy verge, where the tracks of wheels told the educated eye this was where such an engine had stopped before. Divesting herself of her driving rig, she and Gorse exchanged places and a few minutes later, arrived with the utmost decorum at the shiny black rear doors of Viscount and Lady St. Ives' home while in town.

"Thank you, Gorse. See you tomorrow."

"Yes, miss. And may I say, well done."

Glowing, she climbed the scrubbed steps and let herself into the rear hall. To her right, swinging doors opened into the kitchens, already bustling with preparations for dinner, which was served precisely at eight on the evenings her parents were at home. To her left were offices and the quarters of the senior staff. The housemaids had their rooms on the fourth floor. She climbed the stairs to the second level, where cool marble floors gleamed and the scents of wax and the freesias in their Chinese vase on the hall table greeted her in a silent benediction.

There was much to be said for silence. Perhaps Mama had not yet returned from paying her afternoon calls.

"Claire? Is that you?"

Claire's chest deflated in a sigh. It had been too much to hope that she could escape to her room unnoticed. "Yes, Mama."

"I wish to speak to you. In the morning room, please." The tightness in her mother's tone was her first warning. Like the yellow arc on the pressure gauge, it indicated that if something were not done immediately, the consequences could be dire.

The happy glow of a fine afternoon's drive faded. In point of fact, the second brightest spot in this otherwise dreadful day had been the explosion.

Which she had no doubt at all was to be the subject of the next quarter of an hour.

3

Lady St. Ives sat upon the forest-green brocade couch, its width sufficient to accommodate the bustles and petticoats of the fashionable, in the forefront of which she maintained a dashing lead. Her navy-and-white striped silk skirts were overlaid by a polonaise of navy damask trimmed in gold ruching, and gold rosettes drew the eye to a square neckline and the statuesque figure that was the envy of many a dumpier matron.

The fact that Claire had inherited her father's height but not her mother's figure, her father's unruly auburn mane and not her mother's blonde curls, was a continuing source of despair. Only in the last year or two had she given up hope of developing differently than unpleasant reality suggested. The release of that last hope had been painful, contributing directly to her reluctance to be made a show of during the Season.

And speaking of unpleasant reality ...

"Sit down, Claire. How did you enjoy your classes today?"

Was this a trick question, set to trap the unwary? "Very well, Mama."

"So much so that you stayed late?"

She and Gorse had indeed taken a somewhat circuitous route home in order to practice right turns, but not enough to cause alarm. "I'm sorry, Mama?"

"I have just had a tube from Madame du Barry informing me that you did not appear for your appointment at four o'clock."

Madame du Barry. Madame du ... oh. "But the fittings aren't until tomorrow."

For the second time that day, she was pinned in place by an unrelenting blue gaze. "They were today." A narrow brass mailing tube stood on the table, obviously fresh from the vacuum delivery system that snaked beneath London like a veritable Medusa of communication. Lady St. Ives tapped the rolled-up sheet of paper that had come inside it against the palm of her hand. "Do you have any idea how much effort I put into securing your appointment with her? Do you know how sought-after she is? Why, your appointment followed directly after that of Princess Beatrice. *Princess Beatrice*, Claire!"

"I'm so sorry, Mama. I honestly thought it was tomorrow." How could she think about something as mundane as a dress fitting when the day had been such a disaster? A tube from Professor Grünwald could only be a matter of time. She should really be going about in a smock and boots. Think of the wear and tear she might save the stylish efforts of people like Madame du Barry.

"As it is, we will barely be able to get another fitting before your graduation, and I shudder to think what I will do if she decides to stop work on your presentation gown. Honestly, dear, is it so difficult to keep important things in mind? You are such a twitterpate sometimes—I really wonder if your education at St. Cecelia's is having any effect at all."

"I'm getting top marks in French and German," Claire offered meekly.

"That will serve you well should you need to direct a staff in those languages. But in order to have a staff, you must have a home of your own. To have a home of your own, you must attract a husband of wealth and standing. And in order to attract a husband, you must yourself be attractive. How can you do that if you miss appointments with your modiste?"

Claire hoped her future happiness did not depend solely on a designer's skill with tapes and drapery. "I would hope the man I marry would be attracted to my mind, not the efforts of my dressmaker."

"Don't be impertinent. I am quite serious." That, sadly, was true. "You know Papa frowns when you talk like a Wit." But Papa was not here. He had been spending long hours in the House of Lords, arguing with people about investing in the combustion engine.

She supposed gentlemen had to spend their time doing something, but goodness, how foolish.

Mama was speaking again. "... are your dance lessons progressing?"

"The dance master is pleased." Perhaps she could make her smile after all. "Twelve new variations of the mazurka are the rage this Season, and we have all learned them."

"I am happy to hear it. At least I will not have to worry on that account. In the last report I had from your headmistress, she said you actually attain something akin to grace in the ballroom. Perhaps your debut will be a success after all."

Claire gave the expected reply. "I hope so, Mama."

The mother's helper nosed through the open door, its busy brushes cleaning up particles of dirt and dust from both the polished hardwood and the Turkish rug. The size of a loaf of bread and made of gleaming brass, its tiny engine ran on the kinetick energy produced by its perpetual motion. What a help such a device would have been this afternoon.

"Claire, pay attention. I will do all I can to present you to the best society, but it is your charm, your wit, your—" Lady St. Ives seemed to change her mind about the next word. "—your ability to make yourself attractive to eligible partners that will determine your success."

Oh happy thought. "Yes, Mama."

"On that subject, we have no time to lose. We shall begin holding intimate parties for select guests, as a kind of prelude to your debut."

"But Mama, you've said yourself I cannot go into society until after I'm presented." Thank heaven.

"Did I say grand balls? I did not. I said intimate parties here at home, such as the ones I have planned for Friday, Saturday, and Tuesday, and we will of course be part of the progressive dinner on Friday night, after the graduation ceremony. If you had managed to remember your fitting, you would have had new dresses for these occasions. As it is, you will have to make do with something you've already worn, and I hope the new one is ready for next Friday."

Talk of clothes was wearing her out. "I have several pretty dresses, Mama." They were practically new, invitations from Wellesley House and Astor Place having not exactly flowed in.

"I believe the blue satin with the asymmetrical drape and Alençon lace will flatter your eyes and figure the best. This Friday we will have a number of young people in for supper and cards." Lady St. Ives rose and took a piece of paper from her escritoire. Sensing her movement with the statick repulsion that kept it from bumping into furniture, the mother's helper swerved to avoid her feet. "Look over the guest list and tell me if you wish to add anyone. Your papa may have to leave the card party before supper, so we must make up our numbers."

Claire scanned the list. Lady Julia Wellesley. Miss Gloria Meriwether-Astor. Peter Livingston, Baron Bryce. Lady Catherine Montrose. The Marquess of Blatchley. Lord James Selwyn.

Oh, dear. Except for the last, who was unknown to her and therefore still held out hope for congeniality, the list was nothing short of torture. "You've left off Emilie Fragonard, Mama."

"Darling, I was hoping for someone of the sterner sex. Besides, her great-uncle was an *artist*."

"She is my closest friend, and her grandfather on her mother's side is an earl."

Reluctantly, her mother set pen to paper. "I had forgotten that."

Claire bit back an unladylike snort. Her mother's memory was more reliable than Debrett's, and certainly contained more detail. Debrett's, after all, did not list the annual incomes of the peers and their heirs.

"And if we are only playing cards, I should like to invite Peony Churchill and her mother, Mrs. Stanley Churchill."

Lady St. Ives stared at her. "What an outlandish thing to call one's daughter."

Claire had not actually exchanged more than a few shy sentences with the offspring of her idol. Peony did not mix in the circles Claire's mother encouraged, and word would travel fast if Claire sought her out. However, an invitation to Carrick House might open doors in Chelsea, if she could only get this past her mother.

"The name suits her. She is a girl of a certain ... *avoirdupois*."

"But her family? Her connections? Are they related to the Spencer Churchills?"

"I ... I do not know. It is possible."

"I suggest we find out, then." Her mother laid down her fountain pen and rose from the writing desk.

"But Mama, I should like you to receive her. She must be of good family, or she would not be going to St. Cecelia's."

"Not so. There are far too many offspring of engineers and explorers trying to enroll in that school. It is only a matter of time before money and dubious accomplishment gains entrance to doors that have before only opened to breeding. I'm really rather glad that it is your last year there."

"Please, Mama. It is only two ladies. Surely they will not set our party at odds."

"I shall find out if they are connected with the Spencers. If they are, I will welcome them gladly."

And if they are not ... Claire heard the words as clearly as if they had been spoken aloud. Even if Claire begged her on her knees, she doubted Lady St. Ives would receive a woman who had helped to map the Niger River, and whose discoveries of diamond deposits in the Canadas had set the South African financiers of the City on their collective ear. She would not be permitted to even speak to Peony Churchill in the corridors at school, and all her tentative efforts to that end would be for naught.

Frustrated, Claire bit her lip and changed the subject to one that would please her mother. "And how is my little brother today? Has he managed to speak a complete sentence yet?"

Lady St. Ives' features lost their pinched look and softened into a smile. "He has indeed. His nanny tells me she has never seen such a forward child."

"I shall go see him at once."

Her fingers had barely touched the door handle when her mother said, "Claire?" She turned. "What is that in your hair?"

If only she'd gone to see the baby before this interview! Then she could have passed it off somehow on him. "It is dried infusion of dandelion and burdock, Mama. I had an accident in Chemistry of the Home."

Lady St. Ives sighed and followed her to the door. "What am I going to do with you? Come and see your brother. It seems you are only fit to play with babies."

Claire could think of worse ways to spend an evening. Writing one hundred lines, for instance. What a lucky thing that Emilie had perfected her Multiple Nib Scrivener for this very purpose. With as many as ten pens affixed to an adjustable arm, Claire only had to write Professor Grünwald's odious sentence ten times.

Thank heaven for friends who could be depended on.

"I'm so pleased to have been invited, Lady St. Ives." Emilie sounded breathless as she allowed the maid to take her coat and dipped a curtsey to Claire's mother. Perhaps Emilie's corset was laced too tightly. Or perhaps it was merely because invitations did not come her way that often.

"We are pleased you could come." She even sounded as if she meant it, though Claire would expect nothing less from her mother, whose manners were impeccable.

She gave her friend a hug and whispered, "Thank heaven you're here. I couldn't bear it otherwise. We're partners for bridge."

Emilie allowed herself to be steered into the parlor, while Claire braced herself to greet the next arrival.

Lady Julia greeted her as if they were best friends, as did Lady Catherine. Feeling as false as Julia's chignon, Claire pasted on a smile and kissed the air near their cheeks. They would all be taking the stage at Covent Garden at this rate.

"What an unusual gown, Catherine," she said with complete sincerity, taking in the pink silk creation trimmed within an inch of its life. One could hardly see where the dress left off and Catherine began. "Is it new?"

"Delivered just this afternoon, in fact," Catherine said, obviously pleased at the compliment. "I love Madame du Barry's creations, don't you? And these rows of lace trim—are they not the very latest?"

"Indeed," Julia murmured. "Claire, I believe you wore that blue to the Countess of Inglewood's tea last month, did you not?"

Claire was saved from a reply by the arrival of a tall young man who caused the melee in the hall to cease for all of five seconds while the young ladies measured his eligibility from head to foot.

"Lord James Selwyn." Penwith announced him and took his top hat and stick before the young man bowed to Claire's parents.

"I am delighted to see you both again. It was such a pleasure to meet you at Lady Belmont's ball." His hair was close-cropped and reddish-gold, and he wore a neatly trimmed beard that gave him a slightly rakish air. With such a twinkle in those hazel eyes, Claire could almost see him with a gold earring and a cutlass.

"Selwyn." Viscount St. Ives shook his hand, and the newcomer kissed the back of Lady St. Ives's white kid glove as if he were a cavalier from a bygone age. When Claire and the other young ladies had been introduced, the viscount said, "Please join us in the parlor—I believe our party is now complete. I must be on my way to—"

"Not quite, Papa," Claire said. "Mrs. Churchill and Peony have yet to arrive."

"Peony?" Lady Julia looked over her shoulder, interrupted, Claire was certain, in the very act of slipping a chummy hand into the crook of Lord James's elbow as they entered the parlor together. "Peony Churchill is coming?"

"She accepted my invitation," Claire said. "I hope they are able to come."

"Really." Julia glanced at Catherine and Gloria. "How endlessly entertaining." The little group closed ranks around Lord James and moved into the other room, already whispering.

Claire had an uncomfortable ten minutes while playing the hostess, offering her guests tea and lemonade as they made small talk before dinner. Would Peony and her mother come at all? If they did, would Julia and the rest behave, or find some way to embarrass Peony to the point where she would never speak to Claire again? When the doorbell finally rang, she wasn't sure whether to be relieved or even more anxious.

She took Peony's camel coat with its arabesques of black soutache braid herself, and handed it to Penwith. "I'm so glad you could come." Peony's fingers were warm in her own, her dark hair piled high in a Roman-esque coronet, her black-eyed gaze missing nothing. "And your mother?" She glanced behind her, but Penwith had already closed the door.

"She sends her regrets. A matter came up in Parliament and she had to organize a protest at the drop of a hat."

Oh, my. Her admiration for Mrs. Churchill grew in direct proportion to her hope that Lady St. Ives had not heard. "Well, you are here and of that I'm very glad. What a stunning dress." The brocade, a deep wine red most unsuitable for an unmarried girl, was cut so cleverly plain that it could only have come from one place. "Is it from the American Territories?"

"What a good eye you have. Yes. Mama had it sent from New York on the transatlantic airship. She says I must have at least one new dress for this Season. It's a good thing I know she's not trying to marry me off."

"Lucky you," Claire breathed before she could stop herself. "I mean—that is to say—won't you come into the parlor?"

She introduced Peony to her parents, careful to mention that Mrs. Churchill had been unavoidably detained without giving details. Her mother then took over the introductions, standing in Mrs. Churchill's place as she made Peony known to the gentlemen. Out of the corner of her eye, Claire watched as her mother led Peony over to the trio of girls on the sofa.

"Are you to make your bows in two weeks, then, along with the other girls?" A male voice made her jump, and she turned to see Lord James in front of her, turning a crystal glass of something amber in his fingers.

Peony said something, and the girls tittered. "I—yes, I am." Oh, dear. Did Peony need help? She cast around for a polite way to get rid of him. Small talk usually worked. "Are you but recently come to Town?"

"I've been here since Easter. I'm involved in a matter of business that may take me to the American Territories in the autumn."

"Oh?" What was Lady Julia saying now, with such a smile?

"Yes. My business partner and I have a scheme to—"

"I do beg your pardon, Lord James. Miss Churchill has nothing to drink. She will think me a poor hostess."

With another smile, he bowed and turned to speak to Peter Livingston, who was all of nineteen and some kind of relation to him, though how her mother had ferreted that out was a mystery. Claire crossed the room to the punch bowl and ladled some into a cup.

"Lemonade, Peony?"

"Thank you."

Lady Julia smiled with the soulless precision of an automaton. "I was just saying to Peony how trim this cuirass cut makes her look. And dark colors, you know, fool the eye into believing one's weight is less than it is."

"As opposed to overtrimming, which increases the silhouette by several inches at least," Peony said with lazy good humor. Lady Catherine turned pale and looked down at her pink bodice.

"Did you make your dress?" Gloria inquired. "Such skill. I compliment you."

"Your compliments are misplaced, I'm afraid. My mother ordered it from New York. I thought you might have recognized the designer, since you appear to be wearing one of his creations yourself."

"Ah," Lady Julia said. "The American Territories." The very tone of her voice suggested that Peony's gown had been constructed by savage tribes, somewhere on a trackless plain. "Mrs. Churchill, I hear, has many connections there. Though not with families such as dear Gloria's, I believe?"

"She has friends all over the globe," Peony said. "It's difficult to keep track."

"My mother beckons us," Claire said desperately. "Shall we go in to dinner?"

Lady St. Ives, much to Claire's relief, had placed Julia between Catherine and Blatchley, and Gloria next to Lord James, who spent the entire meal talking with her about the American Territories. That left Claire between Peony and Peter, with Emilie on his other side—a happy situation indeed. The only person in London who knew Emilie harbored a certain *tendre* for the young gentleman was Claire, and so it was no burden at all to leave him in conversation with her and turn her attention to making Peony more comfortable.

Though she certainly did not show signs of discomfort. Rather, Peony seemed amused at the efforts of the other girls to patronize and belittle her. How did one come to be that strong within oneself? Was it all in having a role model like Mrs. Churchill? No, that could not be it. Lady St. Ives was just as strong in her own way, leader of society as she was. Why, she had taken tea with Her Majesty herself with no more than a slight paling of the skin, which only served to make her more lovely. No, it must be something else. And there was no way Claire could ask Peony something so personal, especially not here at the supper table with all these people within earshot.

Besides, what if Peony laughed? Claire could bear any number of things, but not the laughter of someone she admired. The thought of it was enough to make her keep their conversation to very surface subjects, with the result that Peony probably thought her a mindless ninny.

Breaking up into parties of four or six for cards brought no relief. It was not until Peony took the chair next to her that Claire realized what she had in mind.

"Now, then," Peony said, shuffling the cards as expertly as the riverboat captain that Claire and Emilie had sighed over in *Heart of the Mississippi*, a romantic flicker her mother would never have allowed her to watch had she known about it. "Who wants to learn how to play poker?"

"What on earth is that?" Emilie looked puzzled. "Something to do with fireplace tools?"

Lord James leaned in, his polite smile broadening to an honest grin. "It's a card game the cowboys play in the Wild West," he said. "Miss Churchill, you surprise me."

"I shock you, you mean." Peony fanned the cards at him so that they made a rude noise. "Well? Are you going to join me, or will your high principles relegate you to observation only?"

"My principles aren't that high." Lord James snagged the sleeve of his cousin. "Livingston. Join us. Miss Churchill is going to teach us a card game."

"We need something to bet with," Peony said, "since I don't imagine you're willing to part with the contents of your pocketbooks in front of her ladyship."

Claire cast around the room. "Will sugar cubes do? Or toothpicks?"

Peony beamed at her. "Toothpicks would be perfect. And we need one more player."

"I'll join you." Gloria, who was clearly not letting Lord James out of her sight even for the space of a card game, seated herself gracefully in the remaining chair, her cream silk skirts pooling around her in a casually studied manner.

Claire fetched a silver box full of toothpicks, and Peony explained the rules as she dealt the cards. Hm. It didn't sound too hard. The point seemed to be less what was in one's hand than in how one presented oneself to the rest of the players. Claire might not possess many skills, but putting a good face forward, no matter how she felt, was one of them.

Before long, the stack of toothpicks in front of her was nearly as substantial as the one in front of Peony. "Miss Trevelyan, you have cleaned me out." Lord James laid down his cards. "I salute you and pass."

Since Gloria and Livingston had declared themselves out within minutes of beginning, this left only Emilie with an active hand. And even that did not last much longer. Within five minutes, Peony had won, which surprised no one.

"I, too, salute a worthy opponent," she said to Claire with a smile. "Beginner's luck?"

"I think not," Livingston put in. "Not for so sustained a period. She almost had you."

"She did," Peony nodded. "Shall we play again?"

"Indeed not." Julia materialized behind Lord James's shoulder. "Gloria, Lord James, I claim you both for my table and a hand of Patience."

Lord James rose without complaint, but as he pushed in his chair, his rakish gaze met Claire's. "I look forward to a rematch," he said. "Perhaps it was a case of luck, not skill."

Claire looked him in the eye. How dared he cast aspersions on her ability in her own parlor? "A lady of resources makes her own luck. Do you not agree, Lord James?"

He laughed and tapped the back of the chair with his palm, as if it were the invisible shoulder of a companion. "She does indeed, Miss Trevelyan. She does indeed."

5

"I met a girl this evening."

Andrew Malvern, B.S., R.S.E., looked up as his best friend, still in black tie, walked into the laboratory that filled the entire loft of their warehouse. "You are always meeting girls. Come over here and tell me what you think of this."

Selwyn joined him and leveled his appraising gaze at the tempered glass chamber with its brass fittings and tubing. "Andrew. It looks exactly the same as it did yesterday when you showed it to me. And she wasn't just any girl. She was St. Ives's daughter."

"It isn't the same." Andrew flipped up a lever and ten pounds of coal rattled down a flume and into the chamber. "Look, from here I can control exactly how much current passes through the coal, and how much gas. I've been waiting all evening to show you."

"I was delayed by a game of poker."

Poker? Andrew focused on James's twinkling eyes. "I thought you said you were going to Carrick House for supper and cards."

"I did. And a little baggage called Peony Churchill taught a few of us how to play. She says she learned in the American Territories but I find that very hard to believe."

"Peony? Not Isabel Churchill's daughter?"

"The very one. In Viscount St. Ives's sacrosanct parlor, no less. Isabel, regrettably, was not there, or you could have read about the resulting fracas in the Times tomorrow."

"We may yet. I've already had a tube from Cadbury at the Royal Society of Engineers about the demonstration this evening at Whitehall. Apparently there is unrest among the good English folk who have invested their life savings in the Persia-Albion Petroleum Company. The Peers could barely get past the door to vote."

James snorted. "Fools. Their feeble combustion engines are too unstable, and no one can seem to make them otherwise, no matter how many exhibitions they put on at the Crystal Palace. Steam is the technology that will continue to power the world."

"Which is why I draw your attention to this chamber." He handed James a pair of goggles with lenses shaded to a deep brown. "Put these on and watch."

Andrew put on his own goggles, then pressed two levers. The chamber began to hum. When he pulled on a third, a thin stream of green gas entered the chamber from the top, which condensed to a solid immediately on contact with the coal. The hum intensified and suddenly a brilliant flash exploded within, as though lightning had been generated from the walls of the chamber itself.

In point of fact, it was pure electrick current. "You see? The powerful charge forces the gas into the coal, enhancing its combustion power." Andrew allowed the chamber to power down, and reached in with a gloved hand to retrieve a piece of the supercharged coal. "Put this in a boiler, and you'll only—"

The piece of coal crumbled to bits.

James peered at it, then removed the goggles to look even more closely. "Is it supposed to do that?"

Andrew's hand closed in a fist of frustration. Through the leather, he could feel particles of coal grinding together in his palm. "Of course it's not supposed to do that. All my calculations indicated the gas would harden the coal, enhancing its propensity to burn longer, thus allowing the steam trains to travel further before taking on more."

"I'd have another go at those calculations."

Andrew struggled to conceal the disappointment and—yes—humiliation warring inside his belly at this ignominious conclusion to an experiment he'd been working on for weeks. "Are you laughing at me?"

"Indeed not." He put an arm around Andrew's shoulders. "I haven't your talent for figures and phys-

ics. I'm just the idea man and the financier of this enterprise. We'll find the correct combination of elements,
never fear."

"I know we will." Andrew's shoulders slumped while
he regarded the recalcitrant chamber. "But time is of
the essence. The world is moving quickly."

"I have complete faith in our ability to match its
pace, Andrew. This invention will make our fortune.
Every steam company and builder of trains will be on
our doorstep, clamoring for a license for this process.
Every railyard will have a man educated in how to op-
erate the equipment. Why, these chambers will become
so vital to the railroad industry that entire companies
will be formed just to manufacture them."

Andrew allowed himself a moment to take in the
grand vista of James's vision. This was what he needed
in a partner—a man who could see beyond the confines
of a compression chamber to the horizon of a future
limited only by their abilities and dreams.

"You are right." He removed his gloves and laid
them aside, and slipped the lead-lined leather apron off.
His body felt strangely light without its familiar protec-
tive weight. "Come. I will pour us each a drink and you
can tell me about this girl."

The thick planks of the loft floor sounded hollow
under their feet as they walked to Andrew's spacious
office with its single skylight, its ocular aperture filled
now with a frosting of stars. He lit both lamps on the
desk and rolled up a set of drawings for the compression chamber to make room for the bottle and two
glasses from the sideboard.

James poured slightly more than two fingers of Glenlivet and handed it to Andrew. "You look as though you need it, after such a disappointment."

The fiery liquor burned its way down with the fierceness of regret. "I will recover, and, as you say, have another go. But enough of that. I am happy your supper party was a success. Particularly since I had to talk you into it."

"The company of simpering schoolgirls is not usually to my taste," James admitted. "But they are to graduate next week, and be presented the week after. I look upon it rather as a preview showing, without the tedious competition of all the other young bucks. Livingston is family, of course, and Bryce is civil enough. Between the two of them they make one active human brain."

Andrew snorted with laughter and the whiskey went down sideways, causing him to cough. "Bloods, are they?" he inquired when he recovered.

"Tiresomely so. My esteemed cousin is not even aware there is an expedition returning from the Amazon, much less who leads it. And to Bryce, an airship has less meaning passing overhead than a cloud. He views it not as the crowning achievement of human engineering, but simply as something that gets in the way."

"Until he wants to go to Paris." Andrew admired the lamplight through the peat-colored lens of the whiskey. "Then he might view it differently."

"Not he. A coach and a ferry, I'm afraid."

Andrew made a face. "Poor man. Imagine living inside his skull."

"I cannot. Let us return to a happier topic—the ladies. Miss Peony Churchill is a pistol."

"I thought it was the Honorable you were interested in."

"Andrew, you benighted sod, there are girls you look at with an eye to marriage, and girls you look at simply with an eye. For the sheer pleasure of it."

Andrew frowned. "I would not say that in Mrs. Stanley Churchill's hearing. You'll find yourself cleft in two by one of the foreign blades they say she collects."

"I kept my thoughts to myself, never fear. But the baggage is a toothsome eyeful, and that's a fact."

"James, your mother must be rolling in her grave. Do not say such things about a young lady of such a brilliant family."

"She is going to be just like her fearsome mother, I tell you. And if a lady does not want to be talked of or looked at, she should not lead such a public life."

Since when did a life led in the pursuit of knowledge entitle one to be sniggered at like a Whitechapel doxy? "I will not have you speak of Peony or of Mrs. Churchill that way. You know as well as I the latter is a champion of scientific inquiry, and she has the ear of the Prime Minister as well. We would be lucky to attract her notice, James. Why, a word from her could open doors throughout the ranks of better placed—and better funded—men than we."

James had the grace to look abashed. "You are right. I'm sorry." He cleared his throat and poured himself another finger. "But the fact is that Miss Churchill is a most unusual girl. The Wellesley girl and that horse-faced Montrose chit paled in comparison. Looking at the two of them I was reminded of nothing more than a row of meringues, baked in pastel colors and put on display in a confectioner's case."

"But the St. Ives girl? She is not a meringue? I confess I've not heard of her or seen her out in company." Andrew welcomed the turn of the conversation back into more normal channels. He and James disagreed often in matters of physics or chemistry or philosophy, but not in matters of the heart.

Come to think of it, he could not remember ever having discussed matters of the heart with him before. A strange and sensitive topic, to be sure, and one not amenable to the tromping feet of careless and inexperienced men. Surely such territory belonged to women better equipped to explore it.

"You? Go out in company?" James scoffed. "If a lady doesn't come to a lecture or take a stroll through the exhibitions at the Crystal Palace, you wouldn't know she existed." Andrew acknowledged the truth of this with an inclination of his head. "Miss Claire Trevelyan could be something to look at if she grew a spine and possessed some decent conversation," James went on. "Fortunately, both faults can be easily rectified. In fact, I believe she hides the latter out of fear of her redoubtable mother. But what really drew my attention was the fact that she beat me at poker."

Andrew raised his eyebrows. "Did she, now? How unladylike of her."

"The young lady is a regular card shark. And on her first attempt, too. This leads me to believe there must be a mind lurking behind those big gray eyes."

"If you are noticing the color of her eyes, my dear friend, there is no hope for you." Andrew put down his empty glass. "Allow me to be the first to offer you my congratulations."

Lord James Selwyn knocked back the last of his whiskey and grinned. "All in good time, Andrew. Like a perfect peach ripening upon an espalier, these things cannot be rushed."

Andrew thought of his compression chamber, cold and thwarted, behind him in the laboratory. As always, James was right. But time was as precious a commodity as money, these days. In fact, as far as he was concerned, they were one and the same.

6

The sun beamed down upon Claire's face like a bene-diction—one that would cause an unfortunate outbreak of freckles if she did not get off this stage in the next five minutes.

"The Honorable Claire Trevelyan, firsts in mathe-matics and languages, and the winner of Her Royal Highness the Princess Alice's medal for best essay in German!"

Claire stepped forward to shake the hand of the dean of St. Cecelia's, and took the leather-bound folder that held her diploma. At last, the precious sheet of vellum was hers, with its red wax seal bearing the school's crest. Around her neck, the dean hung a gold medal the size of a guinea on a purple ribbon. It settled against her chest, heavy as validation. She doubted that Princess Alice had actually read her essay, which was an examination of Herr Emil Brucker's new design for a four-piston steam landau. But it was most gratifying to have won, and to see the pride on her mother's face as she and young Nicholas's nanny watched her descend the stairs and make her way back to her seat in the front rows of chairs arranged on the school lawn.

Her father was supposed to be here. Half the reason she had written about the steam landau was so that he would be tempted to read her prizewinning essay, be astounded at the depth of her knowledge, and allow her to drive his landau with his full permission. She had trodden a long and difficult road of umlauts and consonants and polysyllabic compounds, all for nothing.

But no. A lady of spirit did not despair. There was always tomorrow, when surely she could prevail upon him to take a moment to read the essay, even if he hadn't seen her receive the medal. She could always wear it down to breakfast.

When the ceremony finally ended—Lady Julia having taken the seniors' prize for congeniality and Emilie having captured the overall academics trophy—she joined her mother and was enveloped in a perfumed hug.

"I am so proud of you, dearest," she said, pulling back to look at Claire as though she hadn't seen her in years and was surprised at how much she'd grown. "I had no idea you'd written an essay in German."

"You can read it if you like. It's about—"

"Heavens, dear. French was bad enough for me. German was insurmountable. I congratulate you."

"I hope Papa will read it. I had hoped he would be here."

A shadow passed across her mother's face. "Your papa is detained in the Lords. He has been spending many long hours there, working for the good of the country, for which you should be proud of him and not wishing him here for your own selfish reasons."

Claire did not think that wishing one's parents to see one's graduation was so very selfish. Well, perhaps only a little. "I hope when I graduate from the university he will be able to come."

"I'm sure he—what?"

"The university, Mama. I would like to attend Oxford in the fall and study one of the sciences." That was a very vague way of putting it. Claire wanted to study engineering.

Lady St. Ives stared at her as if she'd never seen her before. "What nonsense is this, child?"

Perhaps she should have led up to this more gradually. Spent some time softening her mother up and getting her used to the idea. But since academics were in the air and it was such a happy day, the words had popped out before she had a chance to consider them more carefully.

Considered or not, words failed her altogether at the sight of her mother's face.

"You will put such ridiculous ideas out of your head at once. You are to have your Season, accept a suitable young man, and be exchanging wedding vows by autumn." She seized Claire's arm while the nanny, carrying her baby brother, trailed them across the lawn. "University. Great Caesar's ghost. What outlandish thing will you shame me with next?"

"There is no shame in a university education," Claire persisted with the sinking feeling that she spoke her words into the ether, to vanish forever. "I do not wish to be married so soon. I wish to have a career, like—"

"Like whom?" At the gate, Lady St. Ives rounded on her. "Like that Churchill creature?"

"Mrs. Churchill is admired by civilized people on three continents," Claire said as steadily as she could.

"Isabel Churchill is a self-aggrandizing, grandstanding woman who deserted her family and prospects to go gallivanting into the wilderness with other people's money. I will not permit you to use her as a model for success in the feminine sphere."

Claire fell back a step, as if the very words had slapped her.

"You may well be shocked. She is a Wit of the very worst degree, and I very much regret receiving her daughter into our home last week. She is not related to the Spencer Churchills at all. I had been misinformed."

"You just don't like her because she's not a Blood."

"Do not speak as if you were a silly schoolgirl any longer. Come. We must get you home in time to dress for your reception and the salon at Wellesley House this evening."

Mutinous, Claire nearly refused to walk any further next to the woman who had foiled all her hopes as carelessly as she might swat a fly. But if she did, she would only have to walk home, and half a mile in heeled dress slippers would be at least as painful as riding home in the carriage across from her ladyship.

She was still fuming as Silvie, her mother's lady's maid, helped her out of her afternoon dress and into her new dinner gown. The last thing she wanted to do was pretend she welcomed anyone to such a backward house. Her parents lived in the previous century, that was all. They couldn't help it if the things they lived by—blood, breeding, birth—had become an anachronism in the face of the power of the human brain.

Society had divided itself into Bloods and Wits—the former headed by the Prince of Wales and the latter by the Prime Minister, Mr. Leonard Darwin, son of the famous naturalist—and where one rose to prominence, it was only natural that the other should fade to irrelevance.

The thought of her mother being irrelevant and not even knowing it was some source of amusement, at any rate.

This was cold comfort when Claire had to stand next to her and receive their guests. A harpist had been hired and there would be dancing later at Lady Julia's home, though the affair was called a salon to forestall the gossips from making comments about Lady Julia and her classmates attending a ball before they had been presented. In the meantime, similar parties forming a progressive dinner were going on all over Mayfair and Kensington, the graduates flocking from one house to another to sip lemonade here, nibble an hors

d'oeuvre there, fill a plate with iced cakes and maca-
roons yet somewhere else.

Only another hour, and she and Emilie could flit off
as well, and during the short walk to Wellesley House
she could unburden herself in detail to her best friend.

"Formulating another strategy to beat all comers at
poker?" A male voice rumbled behind her, and Claire
turned in surprise.

"Lord James."

He bowed and extended his hand. "My best wishes
to the new graduate." When he straightened again, his
lashes flickered. "And congratulations are in order, I
see."

"Thank you." She fingered the round gold wafer sitting just below her clavicle, which Lady St. Ives had
insisted she wear, and resisted the urge to take it off
and tuck it in her bodice. She was wearing her very
first low-necked gown, courtesy of Madame du Barry,
and she was not yet used to the way gazes felt on naked skin. "It's the Princess Alice medal for an essay I
wrote in German."

"How very clever. *Ich spreche nicht Deutsch gut.*"

"Neither do I, but the committee evidently thinks I
write it fairly well."

He laughed, and turned to regard the company moving from the sitting room, where the beverages were
laid out, to the buffet in the music room, which was
large enough to accommodate the silken, chattering
company now that the piano was moved back against
the wall.

"And are you enjoying being queen of the day?"

"Not particularly." She caught her breath. If there was anything Lady St. Ives had drilled into her head, it was that in making social conversation with gentlemen, one did not voice one's true opinions unless they concerned the weather, music, or classical literature. And sometimes, depending on the gentleman, not even then.

Again, Lord James laughed, though Claire had not meant to be amusing. "And why not? One would think having a party in one's honor would be most enjoyable."

Claire smiled a public smile. "Of course it is. I am enjoying myself immensely. I simply meant I am not particularly a queen—of a day, an hour, or even a minute."

He took her hand in his. "Perhaps not. But speaking with you has certainly crowned this minute, this hour, for me. I shall live in the glow of it for the rest of the evening."

She blinked, unsure how to respond, while a slow burn of blood crept into her cheeks. She did not blush prettily, like Gloria Meriwether-Astor or Lady Julia. She blotched.

Claire hated to be made to blotch.

She pulled her gloved fingers from his. "Sir, pray do not voice pretty sentiments that cannot possibly be true on such short acquaintance." She sounded as stiff as her own grandmother, but she could not help it. What she really wanted to say to him could not be spoken aloud in her parents' house. "Excuse me while I see to my other guests."

With a swish of apple green silk, she escaped into the sitting room. Where was her father? Perhaps she could prevail on him to speak to Lord James and impress upon him that she was far too young to receive his attentions, particularly when she was still considered to be in the schoolroom until next week. She would not have believed she would take refuge in such a fiction, when she'd been living for today, leaving St. Cecelia's and its teachers behind and embracing adulthood with joy.

"I haven't seen your father, either," Emilie whispered as Claire pretended to pour her friend a cup of punch so that they could speak privately. "I thought he had promised to be here tonight."

"He did, at breakfast. Mama says he is detained in the Lords, voting on some business important to running the country. But still ..."

"You will only graduate once, and he has missed it," Emilie finished. "But that aside, I have no doubt he would give Lord James the set-down of his life if he were here. Even if he is not, you still have his protection. This is, after all, his house. Selwyn cannot behave like this and expect to be received by good society."

"I shall take what protection I can find if it means not seeing that look in his eye." She paused, then said in a rush, "It made me feel as though I were a naked statue from ancient Greece, frozen and unable to pull my draperies over myself."

"How dreadful." Emilie's eyes held sympathy and the smallest bit of shock. "The man is a cad and your parents will not receive him once they know." She glanced over the room, bright with light from the electtrick chandeliers and scented with the perfumes of girls and the bouquets of white lilies on the occasional tables. "Do I imagine it, or is the crush thinning?"

"We must be between waves," Claire said, thankful for the respite. "Now would be a good time to touch up our toilettes. You do still plan to walk with me to Wellesley House, inelegant as that might be? Papa has the landau and Mama is taking my grandmother and my two great-aunts Beaton in the carriage."

Behind her, the front door slammed. Claire's first thought was that she had offended Lord James so deeply that he had finally worked up enough steam to take his leave. But no, there he was in the music room, by the piano, talking again with Gloria. She hurried into the hall, followed closely by Emilie and Lady St. Ives.

"My lord!" her mother exclaimed as the Viscount staggered across the marble squares of the hall and fetched up against the carved banister of the staircase, his chest heaving. Every lamp had been lit, serving to illuminate a face gone gray and a cravat loose and disheveled. He raked a hand through his hair and Claire realized he had lost his top hat. "Vivian, are you hurt?"

"We're done for," the Viscount croaked. "Persia-Albion's failed. I put everything we had into it and now it is gone." He gasped, as though he sobbed, without tears. "I'm so sorry, Flora. So sorry. For everything."

He stumbled into his study, where he closed the door, leaving both Claire and her mother staring at it as though they'd both seen an apparition called up from some dreadful séance pass right through it. From behind the sturdy, white-painted oak panel, there came the sound of another door slamming.

No. Not a door. Claire had slammed every door in this house at one time or another during her adolescence, and that was not the sound of a door.

It was the sound of a pistol shot.

LADY OF DEVICES

7

The Times of London
June 14, 1889

VISCOUNT PASSES IN TRAGIC MISHAP

In a loss as tragic as the fortunes of those with whom he invested in the Persia-Albion Petroleum Company, Vivian Trevelyan, Viscount St. Ives, left his family bereaved on Friday last. While cleaning his collection of Georgian pistols, he apparently did not realize one firearm had been put away loaded. The discharge killed his lordship instantly.

At the funeral yesterday, a nursemaid carried 19-month-old Nicholas, now the fourteenth viscount, who cried during the service as loudly as if he really had been aware his papa was being laid in the ground. Lady St. Ives, who could be forgiven for ignoring the demands of fashion during such a time of grief, instead was careful to maintain her reputation for taste and distinction in a beaded mourning gown by the House of Elsevier in Paris, and a swansdown-trimmed velvet cloak and hat by Belleville. Her daughter Claire, whose only style is that she is now known as Lady Claire, stood silently at her mother's side for the length of the service.

This reporter does not know the fate of the Persia-Albion Petroleum Company, of which the late viscount was a principal investor, along with several of society's leading Bloods and, some speculate, even Her Majesty. However, disturbing rumblings have been heard regarding the company's solvency. Please see the Business section for more details on this unhappy situation.

On a good day, Claire could pretend that her father was merely away—in the Lords overseeing matters of state, or taking a quick trip down to Cornwall to visit Gwynn Place. The viscount had been better known as a shrewd investor and one of the leaders of London society than as a family man. It was not as if Claire had been close to him. All the same, he was her father, and one of the anchors to her life, and without him the whole household had been set adrift.

On bad days, the only thing that could rouse Claire from the stupor of grief was the knowledge that someone had to answer the landslide of condolences and black-edged correspondence, whose brass tubes had piled up on the salver in the morning room to such an extent that Penwith finally had to fetch a wooden chest to hold them. The new viscount could not do it. And Lady St. Ives was in no shape to do it. Except for her appearance at the funeral, she had not left her room since that dreadful night and from what Claire could learn from Silvie, she had no intention of doing so in the immediate future. Claire counted the family fortunate that she had managed to attend the funeral. Had she not, gossip would have been delighted to fill in the blanks that the Times had so obligingly left open.

The doorbell rang for what seemed like the fortieth time since breakfast, and out of habit, Claire paused on the staircase, halfway between curiosity and duty.

"I'm sorry, miss, but the family is not at home," Penwith intoned. He must be so tired of mouthing the same words time after time. On the other hand, at least she did not have to do it.

"But I must see C—er. Lady Claire," came Emilie's voice, raised in anxiety.

"Lady Claire is unable to receive visitors, miss. You will note the crepe upon our door."

Crepe notwithstanding, yes, she was able. "It's all right, Penwith." Claire hurried down the staircase, her skirts trailing behind her in a welter of black silk ruching and pleats. "I am always at home to Miss Fragonard." She dragged Emilie into the morning room and hugged her fiercely, the unshed tears backing up in her throat. "I'm so glad to see you I can't even express it."

"I've sent you a tube every day," Emilie said with the merest tinge of reproach.

"Have you?" Claire released her and indicated a second pile of tubes on the escritoire, which was reaching the limits of its stability, too.

"Oh dear." Emilie appeared to do a quick calculation. "There is two weeks' worth of writing replies between here and the hall."

"At least. I can't bear to think of it."

"Think instead of the kindness of all your family's acquaintance," Emilie said gently. "They wish you to know they're thinking of you."

"I know," Claire took a letter out of a tube on top of the stack and smoothed it flat. "And I appreciate it. I do. But what do I say to everyone? No one really believes what the Times said and we don't dare refute it."

Emilie took the letter from Claire's hands. "They would not be so crass as to speak it aloud. Stick to the main point—their condolences. And for that I have just the thing. Have you forgotten my Multiple Nib Scrivener?"

"You're assigning me lines?" Was this meant to take her mind off her situation?

"No, you goose. Where is your mourning stationery?" She rustled through the pigeonholes of the escritoire. "Never mind, I have it. We line up the reply cards like so—" She laid them out like dominoes and seated herself at the table. The ten nibs of her device hung poised above the creamy stationery. "—and begin composing. What would you like to say?"

"What would I do without you?" Claire gathered her wits and tried to remember what she and her mother had done when Grandmother Trevelyan had gone to her eternal reward. "We so much appreciate your kindness during this painful time," she began slowly. Emilie's nibs scratched along, following her. "The viscount, Lady St. Ives, and I are thankful for your thoughts and trust that God will keep us in His hand."

"Is His capitalized?"

"Yes."

"'... hand.' Anything else?"

"No. Hand them to me and I'll sign them. Fortunately we use the same ink. India Black."

Emilie gave her a look over the rims of her spectacles. "Was that a joke?"

Claire winced. "No, I'm sorry. Merely bad taste."

"I think it's good. It's a sign that maybe in time you'll recover."

"I suppose I will. And Nicholas will be fine, except for the tragedy of his never knowing Father. Never learning how to ride with him like I did. Never seeing him come in at dinnertime and running into his arms, as I did." She reached into her sleeve for her damp handkerchief.

"But you can teach him how to drive the steam landau when the time comes." Emilie's eyes were soft with understanding, and Claire hung onto her self-control with difficulty.

"That's true," she said, swallowing the tears down. "That much I can do." She picked up the next batch of tubes and began extracting their contents. All she had to do was reverse the address on each tube and pop a reply in. Emilie deserved to have won the all-around academic award. She was brilliant. "At this rate we could be finished by teatime, just in time for the next mail."

"It almost makes you wish you had no acquaintance, doesn't it?" Emilie bent to her task.

"Almost." Claire directed her attention to the pile in earnest.

8

The offices of Arundel & Hollis, Solicitors, were nearly as posh as the prime minister's house, in Claire's informed opinion. A clerk guided them to a heavily carved oak door whose brass plate identified it as belonging to the corner suite of Mr. Richard Arundel. A man of rather more dashing years than his position might suggest came out of it and greeted Lady St. Ives, bowing in his beautifully cut Savile Row suit.

"My heartfelt condolences upon your loss, my lady," he said, clasping her black-gloved hand in both his bare ones. "I am so glad you saw fit to call upon us in this difficult time."

Since they were there for the reading of her father's will, Claire thought this was going a little far, but of course she said nothing.

Mr. Arundel guided them over to a pair of arm-chairs upholstered in glossy burgundy leather and studded in brass, placed strategically beneath a huge map of the Empire. He ordered the clerk to bring tea, and when it arrived, he invited Claire to pour. When she had handed the cups around, he took a sip and began.

"His Lordship entrusted the bulk of his business dealings to this firm, as well as his personal instruments. Following the reading of the will, I am happy to be in a position to apprise you of your situation—would it be appropriate to do so now, or should I wait for a more convenient time?"

Beneath the shroud of her black *point d'esprit* veil, Lady St. Ives's head drooped. On her knee, her tea in its delicate Sèvres cup cooled, untouched.

Claire cleared her throat. "Mr. Arundel, my mother's spirits may be taxed by such an apprisal, but I assure you it is necessary. This morning we were accosted by a number of dunner-men at our very door. It's imperative we learn of the state in which my father left his affairs so we can end such nonsense."

Mr. Arundel eyed her, then Lady St. Ives. "Very well. Shall we begin?" At her mother's nod, he went on, "His lordship's will is fairly straightforward. Gwynn Place, of course, goes to the infant Viscount in its entirety—lands, house, incomes and rents. Since Carrick House came into the family after the marriage of yourself and the late viscount, it goes to you, Lady St. Ives, with the proviso that it go to Lady Claire upon your decease, even if you should marry again and have, er, issue by that marriage."

Claire had not expected this. She'd thought the lot would go to Nicholas. Goodness. The prospect of a house to depend upon in her middle years—or a refuge now should she prevail and be allowed to go to university—was a gift she had not considered in all her wildest dreams.

"There are, of course, the usual small bequests to the servants, and a marriage portion for Lady Claire when she reaches eighteen years of age in the autumn." Mr. Arundel paused to fold up the creamy sheets of the will. "Which brings me to the next, rather less straightforward part of our meeting today. My lady, are you sure you can bear this now?"

Her mother cleared her throat, as though she was not quite certain her voice would work properly. She lifted her veil and placed it carefully on the wide, heavily decorated brim of her black straw hat. "Quite sure, thank you, Mr. Arundel." Finally, she took a sip of tea.

Claire poured herself a second cup.

"Very well. How familiar are you with the business operations of the Persia-Albion Petroleum Company?"

"Not at all. My late husband was often in the Lords, voting on matters that concerned it, but he did not share his affairs with me."

"Ah. Had you heard, then, of the collapse of what they are calling the Arabian Bubble?"

"No, Mr. Arundel." Lady St. Ives passed a hand over her bone-white brow. "Could we get to the point, please?"

"Quite." The lines of sympathy in his face smoothed out a trifle. "The point, then, is that as its principal investor, the bulk of His Lordship's capital was tied up in the Persia-Albion Petroleum Company. He believed deeply in the future of petroleum and its application to the combustion engine. Unfortunately, any and all models of this engine have been failures, and some have even resulted in fatalities. The public, once so enthusiastically in its favor, has turned the tide of its opinion, pulling its support. Two Fridays ago it was discovered that all public shares of the Company were worth less than the paper they were printed on, and the entire enterprise collapsed. Your husband's capital, and that of the other investors, has gone to pay the public debt. In short, my lady, it appears that you will have no source of income to ease your widowhood."

"No source of income." Impossible. "What about Gwynn Place? Our family has been living on the income from that for centuries."

"Your father mortgaged it to invest in the P.A.P.C. When all the debts are settled, you will be fortunate indeed to have the house itself. I have already been approached by prospective buyers for the land."

Lady St. Ives lifted her head. "Mr. Arundel, I may be Londoner born and bred, but even I know that an estate without its lands cannot support itself. I forbid you to sell any property attached to Gwynn Place. It is my son's heritage."

He inclined his head. "Very astute of you, my lady. That will mean, of course, that Carrick House will have to be sold immediately."

The bottom dropped out of Claire's stomach. "How soon is immediately?"

"By month's end. You did say you wished the importunities of the dunner-men to stop." He smiled, but at the same time, Claire detected real concern in his gaze.

"I appreciate your honesty, Mr. Arundel." She straightened, and put the cup of tea on the low mahogany table between them.

"If we sell Carrick House, the mortgages against Gwynn Place will be repaid?" Lady St. Ives asked.

"I cannot promise that. As you can imagine, many find themselves in the same straits at this time, and there will be many houses for sale shortly. But I could negotiate with the banks on your behalf, and do what I can."

"Thank you, Mr. Arundel. We are in your debt."

Claire winced at this unfortunate choice of words. "What is your advice for the immediate future, Mr. Arundel?"

"Public opinion is running rather high at the moment, I fear. It would be prudent if you were to take some time in the country during your bereavement. No one would think it out of the ordinary, and to be blunt, there may be riots."

"Good heavens." The blood drained from Claire's face, leaving her skin clammy and cold. "You can't be serious. Riots? In Belgravia?"

"Feeling is running high against the Bloods at the moment. Your personal situation aside, the House of Lords is in a state of chaos. There is even talk of a revolution. It would be very, very wise to quietly pack up Carrick House, dismiss the staff, and board the Flying Dutchman by the end of the week, if you can possibly do it."

Claire wished that she had not insisted on being laced quite so tightly this morning. She was finding it difficult to breathe.

"The end of the week?" How was it possible that the life she knew, the life she had taken so completely for granted, could be over by the end of the week? And it was already Wednesday. "We cannot possibly vacate Carrick House that quickly."

"Then I recommend you pack as you would for a tour of the Continent, and board that train regardless." His gaze held hers in all seriousness. "For his infant lordship's sake alone, if for no other reason."

"You are right, of course, Mr. Arundel." The snap had come back into her mother's eyes at the mention of Nicholas. The lioness, it was clear, had been roused at last at the thought of danger to her cub. "We cannot win this battle, but we can retreat and retrench, to fight again another day." Claire raised her eyebrows. "I will take Nicholas and repair to Gwynn Place on Saturday at the latest. Claire will stay to oversee the disposition of the furniture and the servants, and follow me by the end of the month, as you said."

"But Mama—" Claire struggled against the current of her mother's will as her choices flew by, every bit as unreachable as the banks of the Amazon. "What about the Season? Being married by the fall?"

"Nonsense. There will be no Season—we are in mourning." Her mother rose, smoothing the crisp black figured silk of her skirts. The beading on her bodice winked in the lamplight, for Mr. Arundel had the velvet curtains drawn against the morning sun. "Mr. Arundel, I assume I may distribute my husband's bequests for our servants before I dismiss them?"

"You may. But I fear Lady Claire's marriage portion ..."

"... will have to go to pay the debts," Lady St. Ives finished. "I understand. How much was that?"

"Twenty thousand pounds, my lady."

All the breath whooshed out of Claire's body, and she was profoundly thankful she had not yet stood up. Twenty thousand pounds! She could have gone for a master's degree at Oxford with that—and financed an expedition to the Amazon on top of it! And then lived happily in Carrick House, hosting salons and entertaining the leading intellects of the day. How could Papa have done this to them all? It was apparent to even a baby that steam was the technology the world ran on— how could he have been so foolish as to gamble their futures on petroleum? Their very lives?

The image of her father as an all-knowing, godlike figure who controlled the destiny of the nation began to crumble—first his feet, then his legs and trunk, until the last thing to go in her mind's eye was his smile and his crinkly brown eyes.

"Lady Claire? Are you quite all right?" Mr. Arundel bent to look her in the face. "Some more tea, perhaps?"

"No, thank you." She swallowed her anger and struggled for civility. "I'm—I'm just trying to take it all in. It's quite a shock."

"It is, and I am deeply sorry to be the bearer of unpleasant news. But I felt it was better to be honest than falsely solicitous." From the door, Lady St. Ives gazed over their heads, fixed on some uncertain view. The solicitor leaned closer. "Forgive me for making a personal remark, my lady, but I understand you are a young woman of considerable intellect. You might consider taking up a career of some sort."

Claire blinked at him. "You mean ... work? Go into trade? Is it as bad as that?"

The solicitor straightened. "I'm afraid so. Without a marriage portion, you join the already well-populated ranks of impoverished Blooded ladies looking for a secure marriage. At least if you could make your own way in the world you would not have to sail those uncertain waters."

Claire had always wanted to join the ranks of the engineers of the Royal Society, traveling to far-off lands in support of the devices she would invent. Bridges across the wild rivers of the American Territories. Laboratories in India. Roads in South America. But that took money. Without it, her dreams were as fanciful as fairy tales and even less likely to have happy endings.

"But without going to university, what could I do?"

Mr. Arundel looked into her eyes and spoke with conviction. "You are a young lady of spirit and capability. I should begin by closing Carrick House. And then

I should find friends with whom I could take refuge, and begin answering advertisements."

She didn't even know where to look for advertisements. "Thank you. I shall let you know what I decide."

Lady Claire Trevelyan had walked into this office half an hour ago with brains, spirit, and a family fortune. She left it with the first two still intact.

That was something to be thankful for, at least.

Directly upon removing her hat, Lady St. Ives dispatched a tube down to Gwynn Place to prepare the staff for their arrival on Saturday. "Despite what Mr. Arundel suggests, I would rather go to Cornwall by airship," she told Claire, tugging on the bell to summon the housekeeper.

"Mama, you cannot. With as much luggage as a trip to the Continent, the weight charges would amount to a fortune."

"I have never had to concern myself with such a thing, child, and I resent having to think of it now."

Claire thought quickly. "Besides, the public will expect you to go by airship. There could be demonstrations on Hampstead Heath, and I shudder to think what might happen if you took Nicholas there. If you go by train you slip out of town undetected."

Lady St. Ives's eyes narrowed, and for the first time, Claire saw the faintest tracings of lines at the corners. "I will allow no harm to come to my son. Perhaps you are right. We must put Nicholas first, regardless of the inconvenience to ourselves." She glared at Claire as if she had been the one insisting on the airship, but Claire did not protest. She would far rather have the lioness than the defeated, weeping woman who had haunted the viscount's rooms this past week.

Her mother assembled the staff that very noon and delivered the unhappy news to them. She distributed the viscount's bequests and promised everyone, right down to the scullery maid, a letter of reference before the week was out. Only Penwith, two footmen, the nursemaid, and Silvie would go with her to Cornwall.

As the upstairs maid came into her mother's room to light the lamps that evening, Claire paused in her packing, a froth of fashionable evening dresses on the bed beside her. "Mama, Mrs. Morven is staying until we close the house, isn't she? If she isn't, I must inform you that cookery was not my strongest subject."

"Of course. I would not leave you alone in an empty house, prey for every brigand roaming the streets. Silvie, the lavender damask goes next. I shall want it when the year of mourning is up." Carefully, with layers of tissue between each fold, Claire helped Silvie lay the damask in the steamer trunk next to the bed. "Except for those going to Gwynn Place, the staff will stay on until the end of the month. You must send a tube telling us which train you will take and I'll have some-one meet you at St. Ives station with the trap."

Claire took a deep breath, Mr. Arundel's words still fresh in her mind. "I've been thinking, Mama."

"Yes?" Her voice came muffled from the closet.

"I believe I should like to stay in town a little longer."

Lady St. Ives emerged with a fresh armful and handed it to Silvie. "Longer than what?"

"The end of the month."

"Nonsense. The staff are all leaving."

"If we could keep Mrs. Morven on, I could—"

"The black walking skirts should go on top. I shall want them immediately when we arrive." The topic closed, her mother had already returned to the matter at hand, dismissing her daughter as though she were a servant—as though her thoughts and wishes did not matter. Resentment burned in Claire's chest, her corset restricting its rise.

She took the walking skirts from Silvie, placed them on top, laid a layer of tissue on top of them, and closed the trunk. "Mama, I do not wish to go down to Corn-wall right away, I wish to stay in London and look for employment."

A full five seconds of silence passed. Perhaps, in the depths of the closet, she had not heard. "Mama? I said—"

"I heard you." Lady St. Ives emerged with a rack of evening slippers and calling shoes. "This is no time for silly jokes. Save the next trunk for unmentionables, please. Silvie, you may pack them in the morning."

"I am not joking. Mr. Arundel said I was a young lady of spirit, and if I do not want to join the ranks of other Blooded ladies looking for a husband, I should look to supporting myself."

"Mr. Arundel is a liberal-minded fool. I'm surprised your father retained his firm if he harbors Wit tendencies."

"He was only trying to be helpful."

"And you at this moment are not. Please stop this chatter and help us finish. My head begins to ache."

Claire tightened her lips against a sharp retort, and after a moment, relaxed them enough to speak. "If I can find employment before we close the house, may I stay with friends afterward?"

"With whom would you stay?"

"Emilie. Or—or perhaps Julia, at Wellesley House. Goodness knows they have room enough." The Channel would freeze over before she asked Lady Julia for anything, but her mother did not need to know that.

"I'll not have a daughter of mine begging for rooms in the street. Stop this at once, Claire. You'll come down to Cornwall as planned, and I'll do my best to find a suitable match for you once our period of mourning is concluded. It is obvious that your active mind needs to be engaged with the running of a home instead of these wild schemes."

"But I don't want a—"

"Claire." For a moment her mother's face softened into grief. "Please do not talk of separating yourself from me. I cannot bear it. We must stay together. For now."

It was the softening that cooled Claire's resentment into compassion as her own heart reproached her for adding to her mother's burden. "Yes, Mama. For now," she said at last, and turned away to pull in another trunk from the hall.

It was fortunate that *now* was a very flexible concept.

10

The great engine of the Flying Dutchman, capable of eighty-nine miles per hour and therefore making it the fastest train in the world, huffed out an enormous puff of steam at precisely nine o'clock and began to pull slowly away from platform number four at Paddington Station.

Gorse tugged his cap from his head and waved it as Claire lifted a gloved hand. "Good-bye! Safe journey!"

Lady St. Ives, of course, did not lean out of the window, but Silvie did, her elegant black-gloved hands waving with such emphasis that Claire shot Gorse a sudden look of comprehension. "Gorse, is something going on between you and Silvie?"

"Was, miss." He swallowed, his Adam's apple bobbing with sudden effort. "Not so sure about now, though."

"Why on earth didn't you say something? You could have gone down to St. Ives with them instead of the second footman."

"They'll still drive carriages in St. Ives, miss. I'm much more likely to get a place here." His gaze never left the train and the distant black flutter of Silvie's glove. "I have an interview at Wellesley House this afternoon, as a matter of fact. Word is that his lordship is soon to be the owner of a four-piston laudau."

"No! I don't believe it. That family would never give up its horses."

"Times change, miss, as we are living proof." They stood upon the platform until the last of the Dutchman's carriages disappeared around the bend. "Would you like to drive home, miss?"

"No, you may. Perhaps it will help take your mind off Silvie."

"Not much possibility of that." He guided her outside and waited until she had climbed into the landau, proud possessor of only two pistons. Two was all anything but a steambus needed. Four was ostentatious. How fast did Julia's father's driver propose to go? Or— yes, that was it—he obviously planned to enter the races at Wimbledon. She snorted, then resumed watching the road like a hawk on a fence post.

The truth was, after Mr. Arundel's information on Wednesday, she looked at London with new eyes—eyes that saw the unrest, that found menace in a crowd surging to board a bus, that calculated distance now in terms of safety rather than convenience. She was no coward, but all the same, Claire was content to let Gorse navigate the turn into Park Lane and skirt the boundary of Hyde Park, where beyond the trees she could hear the roar of a crowd.

Gorse heard it, too, and applied a little more steam. "Let her stretch her legs a bit."

"There must be a demonstration of some kind."

"Likely the orator of the hour getting folk stirred up."

"Yes, I'm sure that's what it must be."

Her breath did not come easily until they had turned into Wilton Crescent and hurried into the safety of their own mews. Once upstairs, Claire dragged the brass-studded trunk, which she had thus far resisted filling, out of the hall and into her room. A warm coat, trimmed in the latest Art Nouveau vinery. Three sensible dresses in dark colors, and five pretty embroidered white waists. Two walking skirts. Shoes. Unmentionables. Two practical hats and one utterly impractical one that she loved, with its flowers and plumes. Gloves.

She found herself packing the kind of wardrobe, in fact, that she might have begun a university career with. She left Madame du Barry's evening gowns where they hung. The apple green had been burned days ago. Lady St. Ives had not permitted her to see her father's body, but the memories of that night hung on the ball-gown, as ugly and clinging as soot, and she never wanted to see it again.

She tipped up the false bottom of a small traveling case and laid her few pieces of jewelry inside, then covered it with handkerchiefs, her best set of tortoiseshell hair combs, and her Bible with a lock of her baby brother's hair pressed between its pages. Last of all she put in Linnaeus's *Taxonomy of Elements*, her engineering journal, and a set of pencils. If her new status as a career woman allowed her any spare time, she could continue her experiments and sketches in solitude.

Not that that would mean any great change.

The heavy weight of anxiety in her stomach eased a little now that she had done something constructive about the future. It was time to stop wallowing in her own fear and anger and behave as the young woman of substance that Mr. Arundel, at least, believed her to be. Her father may never have held that belief ... Claire swallowed as hot tears sprang to her eyes.

She blinked them back. Look where Papa's beliefs had got him. She was not a fool. She had never hung her future on the traditions of the Bloods, but she had never done anything to prove that she was different, either. If she thought of herself as a Wit, now was the time to show it. She reached for the bell pull to ring for Penwith, and realized a moment later that of course he was no longer there. If she were to make her own way in the world, she must get used to doing even the smallest things herself.

The house seemed even more silent than usual with the absence of the servants. Most of them had gone to the employment agency with her ladyship's departure. Aside from the ubiquitous mother's helper scooting about in the hall, the only two left were Gorse and Mrs. Morven, the cook, whom she found in the pantry, counting jars of jam.

"Oh, hello, miss—er, my lady. I'm just making an inventory in the event the new owners take the place complete."

"I won't keep you, Mrs. Morven. Do you know what Penwith did with this morning's *Times* before he left?"

"He always leaves it on the hall table, miss, in case your lady mother wants it. Of course, with him gone, if you want it, you just need to tell me."

"Thank you, Mrs. Morven. The hall table is fine. I suppose I should look into canceling our subscription."

"I'll ask Gorse to do it. Ah ... miss? Lady Claire?" She turned at the door. "Me and Gorse—we were wondering ..."

"Mrs. Morven, times are changing. We must not be afraid to speak plainly to one other."

The cook fiddled with her apron strings and adjusted the set of her pristine white cap. "We were wondering, miss, how you'd be set were we to take our positions before the end of the month."

"Have you had an offer from Wellesley House too?" The bitterness rasped at her throat.

"Oh, no, miss. I can't abide the nasty biddy they have as housekeeper there. A face like suet pudding and no salt, that one. But young Lord James Selwyn is setting up his own household and has advertised for a cook. It would be light work, seeing as he's single, and I'm ready to tote a lighter load in my golden years."

"Mrs. Morven, your golden years are a long way off yet. But it would be a change to look after a young man instead of all of us. I'm acquainted with Lord James, you know." She paused. "He is a gentleman of humor and, um, wit." And a bit of a cad, but Mrs. Morven would likely not be the target of that.

"Plus he's offering to equal the wages his lordship— rest his soul—was paying me."

Claire saw her chance to even the score. "Negotiate for more, Mrs. Morven. Another ten percent and he can have you by the end of next week."

The cook's flushed cheeks became positively apple-like as she smiled. "You'll be all right, then, miss?"

"I'll be perfectly all right. In fact, I hope to be gain-fully employed by then, myself."

"Beg your pardon?"

"I'm not going down to Cornwall, Mrs. Morven. I'm going to get a job and go to work, and apply to begin at the university in the fall."

"Are you, now, miss?" Mrs. Morven's eyes widened.

"Yes, I am, despite what my mother says. I'm nearly eighteen and I have nothing but a trunk full of clothes, a steam landau, and my brains to recommend me. So I and they are going to work. Which is why I need the *Times*. Would you be so kind as to give me some instruction on how one actually goes about an-swering an advertisement?"

11

What a relief it was to send mail tubes that didn't contain stationery rimmed with black. By Tuesday Claire had arranged four interviews—two families wanted a governess, a scientist wanted a secretary, and the British Museum needed someone to catalogue artifacts.

On Wednesday, she heard from Lady St. Ives.

My dear Claire,

We arrived safely Saturday evening and have settled in to life in the country. We are all well and your brother has gained another two pounds.

Polgarth begs me to tell you that the chickens send their best greetings and look forward to your arrival.

As does your loving
Mama

Claire had to smile. As a child, she had loved the flock at Gwynn Place, which gave the best eggs in the parish. Polgarth the poultryman swore that she had a natural gift with them, and they used to follow her about the garden as if she were an exotic sort of rooster. The companionship of birds may have been all she needed then, but at nearly eighteen her require- ments were substantially more. The hens would have to do without her some while longer.

By Thursday, she had decided that governessing was not the career path she was meant to take—not unless she was desperate and starving in the streets. The gentleman at the British Museum seemed more interested in cataloguing her anatomy than in her quali- fications for cataloguing his artifacts, which left her feeling as though she needed a bath when she left that afternoon. Whatever her father's faults, at least his pro- tection had been real. No man would have dared to treat her that way if he had still been alive.

Of course, if he had been alive, she would not be pi- loting carefully through the crowded streets of London, sweating in her duster and jumping out of her seat every time a horse shied upon seeing the landau. Silly creatures. She made the turn onto the Blackfriars

Bridge and proceeded across it in a stream of drays and carriages. The scientist kept his laboratory in a warehouse on Orpington Close, which turned out to be little more than an alley running down to the mud on the south side of the Thames. She parked the landau at the foot of an exterior staircase, as instructed by tube, and released the valve. Steam hissed into the air like a sigh of relief at their arrival, and she set the brake.

She was just raising her hand to knock at the lower door when it swung open. The apparition within looked as though it had come up from under the sea. Out of its leather helmet snaked a series of rubber tubes, while a pair of glass-fronted eyes stared at her with alien blankness. The rest of it was covered in a leather apron of the sort butchers wore, and the hands reaching for her were encased in leather gloves.

With a squeak, she stumbled backward, bumping hard against the post that supported the staircase. How far was the landau? Could she get inside and get it fired up before the thing caught her?

"Miss Trevelyan? Don't—what are—oh, blast it!" The monster tore its head off and tucked it under its arm. "I'm so sorry. Please forgive me. I forgot that—Miss Trevelyan? Are you quite all right?" A young man with hazel eyes and tousled hair the color of Brazil nuts took off his glove and extended a hand to her. "I didn't mean to frighten you. It would serve me right if you turned and left this moment."

Slowly, she extended her hand. "Is—what is that, sir?"

"It's a gas mask. I devised it myself, you see—so that I could enter a large compression chamber without breathing in the gases. Look, these tubes attach to a flask of air at the back."

"Ah." She craned her neck to see. "Air, you said? Not compressed oxygen?"

A smile dawned, reaching all the way to his eyes. "You've been reading the scientific journals, I see. Last month's *Illustrated Science* article on Dr. Weathering's undersea bell?"

"Yes, as a matter of fact." She tilted her chin. "Not all of us find our entertainment in *Lady's Home and Garden*."

"You'll find neither home nor garden here, I'm afraid. Do come in. Watch your step. These boards are uneven."

She followed him across a huge warehouse containing what appeared to be pallets of various metals and glass, along with an enormous heap of lumber, to an interior staircase that brought them up to a spacious loft. "Am I to assume you are Mr. Malvern?"

He stopped in the act of clearing a stack of diagrams off the chair in front of the desk, and smacked his forehead. "Good grief. You will think me an ill-mannered ass. Yes, I am Andrew Malvern, A.B.D. Member of the Royal Society of Engineers. Part owner of this warehouse and in dire need of someone to keep me organized."

"A.B.D., Mr. Malvern? Is that a new scientific society? The Association of Biological Diversity or some such?"

"No, no. It means *all but dissertation.* I would have a Ph.D. to add to my string of initials if I could only get this da—er, excuse me, this wretched theory of mine to work."

Claire opened her mouth to ask him what was wrong with his theory, and closed it again. He might not appreciate her nose in his business. And anyway, if she got the job, she would find out eventually, wouldn't she? She seated herself in the chair he had emptied, and regarded the blizzard of papers and drawings on the desk. Oak filing cabinets stood against the wall, papers sticking out of the drawers as though they were trying to escape the crowded conditions within. Here and there, instruments and devices held down stacks of drawings and columns of figures on the floor, and the woodbox next to the cast-iron stove was full of still sealed mailing tubes instead of kindling.

He followed her gaze around the room. "You see why I'm in need of an assistant."

"I do, sir. Were I to be your choice, I should start with the mailing tubes and then work in concentric circles in a clockwise direction, from filing cabinets to loose papers."

"Would you?" His chair swiveled as he followed this thought. "I suppose it's as good a method as any."

"What is your field of research, sir?"

His circumnavigation of the loft completed, he folded his hands on the desk and regarded her. He had very nice eyes, with long lashes and a twinkle that was most distracting. "You make it sound so formal. My interests are in the railroad industry at present. I'm working on a way to make coal go further more cleanly, reducing costs and increasing the engines' ability to use it more completely. As it is, there's too much waste without enough return in speed and efficiency."

"Ah."

"Are you familiar with the workings of engines? Was that your landau I saw out there?"

She may not know the first thing about locomotive engines, but the landau she knew inside and out. "Yes, it's a two-piston Henley Dart, with a five-gallon boiler and a top speed of forty-five miles per hour."

"Did you drive it here at that speed? If so, I salute you."

He was teasing her, the rascal. "No, I topped out at twenty. It is very crowded on that bridge."

"What do you say to taking it for a spin? I've never been able to afford such a thing, and the Dart is a very pretty model." His gaze rested briefly on her hair, then moved to her eyes.

Claire shifted in the chair, and checked that the clasp of her pocketbook was firmly secured. "Did you mean to drive it yourself, sir?"

"Heavens, no. I want to expand my sphere of experience, that's all. I've never seen a woman drive. It would be very useful to have an assistant with such skills. Consider it a test—much more useful than handwriting and typing samples, wouldn't you say?"

Below, a door slammed and footsteps thumped across the boards to the staircase. "Andrew, are you here?"

"I'm conducting an interview. Come on up—my prospective assistant may as well know what she's getting into."

"You're interviewing someone?" A reddish head appeared in the stairwell, then the rest of the speaker's frame. Recognition sparked a moment later, and Claire drew a breath of surprise as Lord James Selwyn stepped into the light from the aperture overhead. "Good heavens. Lady Claire, what are you doing here?" He turned to Malvern. "I thought you were interviewing an assistant."

"Lady Claire?" Malvern glanced down at her letter of application, as though puzzled he'd missed this fact.

"We are one and the same." She rose and extended a gloved hand to Lord James. "I thought it prudent to use my family name and not my title in my correspondence. Lord James, this is unexpected."

"Not half as unexpected as you interviewing for a job."

She lifted her chin, even as the hot blood scorched her cheeks. Blast. She would blotch again, and in front of her prospective employer, too. "My circumstances demand flexibility, my lord. And you agreed yourself the last time we met that a lady makes her own luck."

"Making one's own luck is one thing, but reducing oneself to trade is quite another. Is this a joke you're playing on us?"

"James, what a thing to say." Malvern frowned. "Miss Trev—er, Lady Claire. Please excuse my partner's forthrightness. He has been too long in the American Territories."

"Believe me, my circumstances are no joke," she replied in as steady a tone as she could manage, considering her temper was fast approaching a rolling boil. "I am seeking employment, and believe I could contribute to Mr. Malvern's operations here."

"Not to mention the fact that she can drive," Malvern put in. "That's tipping the scale right there."

"Andrew, don't talk nonsense. Lady Claire is a society belle barely out of the classroom. What can she contribute here? What does she know of science or business?"

"If you would address me directly, Lord James, I could tell you that I graduated with firsts in mathematics and languages, and I plan to apply to the engineering program at the university this fall." She enunciated each syllable so crisply that each word cut the air. "This position, besides keeping me in bread and butter, would go far in recommending me to the admissions committee. If that were any of your business, of course, since it is Mr. Malvern who is interviewing me at present."

Lord James stared. "The girl has a spine after all."

Malvern pushed his chair back. "James, what has got into you? Miss Trevelyan, perhaps we should go for that drive now. I don't know what bee my partner has in his bonnet, but it's embarrassing both of us."

"I just find it amusing, Andrew, that the lady who turned down the offer of my regard is now forced to seek employment in a venture I'm financing. I'm merely appreciating the irony of it all."

"What?"

"The offer of your regard?"

Claire and Malvern spoke simultaneously. Then Claire controlled her tongue, gathered her courage, and bid farewell to her hopes. "Mr. Malvern, I regret taking up your time today, but I thank you for seeing me. Good afternoon."

"Wait. Miss Trev—er, Lady Claire. Our interview is not finished."

"I believe it is. If I am to be dependent on the financing of Lord James, then I prefer to seek employment elsewhere. In any case, he does not believe me capable of carrying out my duties."

"But he's not—Miss Trevelyan, wait—"

She reached behind and twitched the hem of her grey suit out of any possible reach of Lord James's patent-leather shoes, and swept down the stairs. Malvern darted after her, but Lord James caught his arm and their raised voices followed her out of the warehouse, muffled only by the slam of the exterior door.

She ignited the landau and drove back to Wilton Crescent as fast as she dared, where she found Mrs. Morven in the kitchen preparing dinner.

"Mrs. Morven. Are you still set on taking employment with Lord James Selwyn?"

"Yes, miss." The cook eyed her disheveled state, for she had not stopped to put on her motoring duster at the warehouse. "Why do you ask?"

"My advice has changed. Ask for twenty-five percent more, Mrs. Morven, not ten. And you have my congratulations and my deepest sympathy should you get the job."

12

Friday brought two more depressing confirmations that governessing was not the career for which she was destined, and Claire began to give serious consideration to returning, hat in hand, to the British Museum. But that, she thought, glancing at the twilight sky, would have to wait until Monday. She ought to just make it home before the street lamps came on.

As she made the turn off Grosvenor Crescent into Wilton Crescent, she heard the same roar as before—as though hundreds of voices were expressing their outrage—at Hyde Park Corner. Pulling into the mews behind Carrick House, she released the landau's steam and listened.

Birds, singing their adieux before dark.

The clash of cutlery from the town house next door, whose kitchen windows were open.

And in the background the roar of a huge crowd, getting louder.

Footsteps. No, an all-out sprint, booted feet slapping on the cobbles, coming down Wilton Crescent as though—

Gorse pelted into the mews, his driver's cap gone and his coat unbuttoned. "Miss! Lady Claire—oh, thank God. They're coming, miss. You must take the landau and run to Miss Emilie's without delay."

Automatically, her hands began the ignition sequence. "What is happening, Gorse? Tell me!"

"It's a huge demonstration at Hyde Park," he panted, the words coming out in chunks. "The Arabian Bubble investors. They're rioting, miss. They swear to loot Carrick House. To get something out of their investment. Now. They're coming here now."

The landau clattered to life and she made sure the brake was set. "Help me get my trunk out of the house. And Mrs. Morven. We've got to get her out, too."

"Miss, there isn't time for possessions!"

"Come on, Gorse!"

But Mrs. Morven had left a note that she had gone to take victuals to the Foundlings' Home. Thank goodness for that. "Gorse, you'll have to go over there and prevent her return."

"As soon as you're away, miss."

They pounded up the stairs. The house was practically naked, with the china, plate, and paintings already on their way down to Cornwall on a dray. The looters would have a tricky time getting the heavy furniture out the doors. With Gorse in front and Claire in the rear, they lugged her trunk and traveling case down the stairs. With a pang, she thought of her pretty bookcases and all her books, which she hadn't got around to packing quite yet. Maybe someday she would come upon them in a stall in Portobello Road, once the looters lost interest in books about biology and engineering.

Wedging themselves through the kitchen door with the trunk, they could hear the sounds of individual voices at the curve of Wilton Crescent. "Hurry, miss. Go and don't look back."

"But you're coming with me!"

"No, miss. I'm going to send a fast tube to Sir Robert Peel's policing force and try to hold them off at the door. If I can't do that, I'll take to my heels after Mrs. Morven."

"Gorse!"

"No arguments, miss. Mrs. Morven and I shall see you at Miss Emilie's." He secured her trunk to the rear with a pair of leather straps, and slapped it twice. "Now, miss! Quickly!"

The first of the rioters poured into the mews and gave a great shout of triumph when they caught sight of the landau. Claire's heart leaped in her chest and she pushed the steering lever out as far as it would go. The rioters closed the forty feet between them in less time than it took to gasp, so that by the time the landau had completed the turn, they were already on her. She gave it some steam and the landau took off like a racehorse at Ascot, bumping over something she didn't want to think about and eliciting a scream of rage. Hands and fingernails scraped at the landau's shiny exterior, sliding off in a cacophony of frustration.

She did not stop to check the damage—or to look both ways at the corner. Behind her, a window broke with a crash and she heard Gorse's distinctive voice turn the air blue as he mounted his resistance. The landau careened into Belgrave Square, causing a pair of roans to shy and paw the air while their coachman shouted obscenities at her, and she swung a quick right, heading for Cadogan Square and Emilie's house. She did not stop at Lowndes Street either, rocketing across it with the throttle wide open and the speed indicator buried at the bottom of its arc.

Heart racing, hands shaking so badly she could hardly grip the steering lever, she slowed to a respectable ten miles per hour in Cadogan Square and coasted to a stop in front of Number 42. After she set the brake and climbed down, she paused. She didn't like to leave the landau in the open street. First order of business was to secure safety with Emilie, she thought as she marched to the door. The second thing would be to find a place in the stable to hide it before some stray looter recognized it and they brought the hounds of hell down on the Fragonards.

A maid answered her ring. "Good evening, Gwennie. I'm here to see Miss Emilie on a matter of extreme urgency, please."

The maid invited her into the hall and vanished upstairs. A moment later she heard the sharp sound of a

voice, quickly muffled, a door slamming in the far
reaches of the house, and then the swish of skirts descending the stairs.

"Lady Claire," Mrs. Fragonard said from the final
turn of the staircase, in tones so civil they practically
cracked and shattered on the marble floor.

Claire looked up. "Mrs. Fragonard, I apologize with
all my heart for descending on you like this, but I must
see Emilie."

"On what errand?"

Claire paused and looked at her more closely. Emilie's mother had never been a beauty, but she had a
kind heart and Claire had been a guest at her table
many times. What was the reason for this carefully
schooled neutrality of feature? This coldness of tone?

"I'm afraid I find myself at your mercy, ma'am. It
seems that a host of—of investors have taken it on
themselves to importune an empty house, and I'm unable to go home this evening. I have my trunk with me,
and I was hoping to beg your hospitality just for tonight."

Not a very gracious speech, but it would have to do.
In her memory, Claire heard her mother's opinion of it.
Well, her mother was safely in Cornwall and only a fool
would have stood on the step begging the rioters not to
make such a fuss.

"My hospitality? After the snub your family dealt
my daughter?"

Claire stared at her, lost. "I'm sorry?"

"Do not imagine I don't know how difficult it was to obtain Lady St. Ives' permission to invite Emilie to your graduation party."

Claire's mouth opened and closed. Then she took a deep breath and tried again. "Ma'am, I assure you no offense was meant by my mother, and I was very glad to see Emilie there. She has been a wonderful friend to me, especially during these past weeks. I beg you accept my apology for anything my family may have done."

Even this pathetic but sincere appeal had no effect. "What they've done? You obviously have no idea how much the Arabian Bubble has cost this family, young lady."

Claire's eyes widened. "You invested, too?"

"We did, and now we are paying for it. I am no penniless rioter, however. If I were, I would also be tempted to, as you say, importune an empty house."

"Mrs. Fragonard, please—if you'd just let me speak to Emilie—"

"Emilie is unable to receive guests at present. I have no personal animosity toward you, Lady Claire, but your parents have my undying disdain. I cannot let my daughter retain her connections with such a family. In this day and age, it is too dangerous. Good evening to you. Gwennie, will you see her out."

Mrs. Fragonard, who had not left her lofty perch on the staircase, turned and made her way up it again. When the maid opened the door, Claire passed her like an automaton. Even when she heard a frantic pounding on one of the upstairs windows, she did not look up. She could not. If she met her friend's eyes, she would break down in the middle of the street, and there was no time. She simply ignited the landau and released the brake.

Yet another sin to lay at her father's door. Her mother's too, if she were honest. How had Mrs. Fragonard found out that Claire had to practically beg Lady St. Ives to invite Emilie to the party? And what a reason to refuse someone a night's shelter! In such dangerous times as these, people should band together to help each other, not throw their friends to the wolves. But then, her father had played the wolf often enough in Parliament, if the papers were to be believed, voting down the rights of prisoners and those being deported to the Antipodes. Human nature would not pause a moment to turn the tables on him and his, as she was witnessing this very evening.

Was Gorse all right? If he came to find her here, what would they tell him? That they had turned her away? Claire cast a glance over her shoulder as she bowled down the square. Should she wait? She must find shelter before it was fully dark, but where would she go? Wellesley House? Astor Place?

Not likely. Then she blinked as an idea struck.

Who would be most likely to take up the cause of the downtrodden and homeless? Why, Mrs. Stanley Churchill, of course. If she could not find shelter with Emilie, maybe Peony would be the better choice. Yes, that was it. She would go to Chelsea immediately, and send a tube from there to Cadogan Square for Gorse. Surely they would give it to him when he arrived. After all, *he* had done nothing to offend.

13

Claire had never been to Peony's home, but she knew it was on Elm Park Road in Chelsea. Once she located the street, finding the house was just a matter of making inquiries—and even that proved unnecessary. Only the house of Mrs. Stanley Churchill would have a band of—Claire peered through the twilight—wild Indians on the front steps?

She parked the landau and made her way up the walk, sidling past the group of children playing on the railings of the white Georgian house. Not Indians. But definitely something wild, as their boots appeared to be made of animal skins. She rang the bell and waited.

To her astonishment, Peony herself peeked through the nine-paned glass and answered the door. "Why ... Claire Trevelyan. What a surprise."

"I'm so sorry to arrive unannounced like this, but I'm in rather a fix and I was hoping to ask a favor of you."

"As long as it doesn't involve funding of any sort, I'm all ears. Come along into the drawing room." Over her shoulder, she tossed a string of unintelligible syllables that made two of the children laugh.

"No, no funding. Who are those children?"

"They are Esquimaux, from the Canadas. Far north of the Canadas, actually. Their band hunts on the land where Her Majesty wishes to mine diamonds. They are here to plead their case before the House, with my mother's help, or they face starvation. Her Majesty wants to boot them off, you see. They're in the way."

"Goodness," Claire said faintly as she seated herself on a striped divan. "And they have brought their children too?"

"They're not very old," Peony pointed out. "Can't very well leave them sitting on an ice floe with a sandwich, can they?"

"I suppose not."

"So what has brought you to us this evening? But first, allow me to offer my condolences on your loss, Claire. I should have said so right away instead of babbling on."

"Thank you."

"How are you managing?"

Claire took a breath and plunged in. "Not very well, I'm afraid. My mother has taken my brother down to Cornwall just in time. There was a riot on Hyde Park Corner tonight, and a crowd of vandals attacked Carrick House."

Peony's red lips fell open. "Good heavens!"

"They're investors, apparently, determined to get something out of my father's estate. As I fled, I heard glass breaking. I hope they find joy in our furniture."

"They'll make a bonfire in the street with it to make their point, more like," Peony said with such world-weary practicality that Claire's skin pebbled with goosebumps. What must this girl have seen in her life? Far more than herself, that was evident. "I'm very thankful that you got away."

"Which brings me to the reason I'm here. You wouldn't have an extra bed for tonight, would you?"

Peony's eyes filled with sympathy. "My dear, I wish we did. But A'Laqtiq and his family have filled all the bedrooms, to the point that the children you saw outside are sleeping under the dining-room table. The carpet is quite thick. All I have to offer you is the bath, I'm afraid. With a bit of ticking it would do in a pinch."

Claire was almost tempted. But it was clear that there were important political issues transpiring in this house, aside from the fact that Mrs. Churchill and Peony probably had enough on their plates hosting an entire foreign delegation. "I couldn't possibly impose on you to that extent, Peony."

"You wouldn't be, truly. Now, if you were to demand my bed and make me sleep in the bath myself, that would be an imposition."

Claire grinned. "It wouldn't come to that. Do not worry on my account. I have friends yet to impose upon."

"I know you do. A girl as nice as you probably has a host of them, all without children under the dining-table. But if you need it, the offer of the bath still stands. Or I could go all out and find a table in a different room to stash you under."

Claire rose, still smiling. "I may take you up on it. Please give my compliments to your mother. I admire her enormously."

Peony took her outstretched hand. "I do, too. If I can be half the woman she is, I'll do well."

"Heaven help Her Majesty's empire in that case."

Peony laughed and escorted her to the door. "I hope to see you soon, Claire." She hesitated. "I would like it if—well, never mind. You have enough to fill your thoughts at present."

Claire could seize an opportunity as well as the next person. "I would like it if we could be friends, despite my mother's opinions on the subject. And since she is eight hours away by train, I think it's safe to say so."

"Let's shake on it. Friends it is." Peony's fingers felt cool and strong.

Claire went back down the walk glowing with warmth. Friends were not so thick on the ground that she would turn one down, especially in circumstances such as these. The loss of Carrick House was a disaster, to call a spade a spade, but in the midst of disaster the good Lord had sent her a blessing. She would never have guessed a month ago that Peony Churchill would offer friendship, unsolicited. But the bathtub notwithstanding, Claire was very glad she had.

In the meantime, here came the lamplighter, climbing down into the chamber under the walk that concealed the engine powering the lamps for this block. While she had been within, full dark had fallen, and Claire had exactly no experience in piloting the landau after dark. Carefully, she opened the switches to the headlamps, and ignited the engine.

Returning home was out of the question. So, the next question became, where should she go? Wellesley House was out. She would rather sleep in a bathtub with no ticking at all than endure Lady Julia's suppressed smiles at her misfortunes. Perhaps she could go to St. Cecelia's and beg the headmistress for a bed. But no, that would entail far too many questions and very likely public exposure of her plight.

There was nothing for it. She was going to have to go to her grand-aunts Beaton in Greenwich, wake them out of a dead sleep, and explain in as little detail as possible why she was there. They were elderly, excitable, and as ignorant as chickens about the affairs of the day. They actually believed that Papa had had an accident while cleaning his gun. Not that that was a bad thing. It was necessary for everyone to at least pretend to believe that, or Papa could not have been buried in hallowed ground. At the same time, giving credence to a lie galled her.

Very well. To Greenwich she would go, and as soon as she read in the papers that the Esquimaux delegation had been heard and were on their way back to their home in the frozen north, she would return to Peony's and claim both friendship and a bed until she could find employment and rooms of her own.

She turned east and tried to visualize the best route. The difficulty with Greenwich was that it lay on the far side of the East End. She could either cross the river at Lambeth and circle around to the south, in which case she would arrive long after midnight, upsetting her grand-aunts even more, or she could stick to the well-populated roads in Town and hope that the speed and the sturdy brass skin of the landau would protect her until she got over the new London Bridge.

If only Gorse were here.

Then again, she thought with a snort as she motored down the Embankment at a respectable thirty miles per hour, she could always accept the offer of Lord James Selwyn's regard. She had no doubt that a fiancée of his would not be chugging briskly through the night, homeless and alone. But then, a fiancée of his would have neither a landau nor a brain to call her own, either.

This cheered her immensely, and she turned her back on the Blackfriars Bridge and took the corner into Farringdon Street with aplomb. Now came the tricky part. The lamp lighters had obviously not come this far yet, leaving her dependent upon her own head lamps to keep her in the center of the thoroughfare. The mouths of the streets yawned black on either side. The sound of the landau's engine bounced back at her from the brick and wood surfaces of the buildings and the cobbles of the street, making it sound as though she were three or four engines, not just one. She swerved to avoid men loading kegs on to a cart, and steered back the other way to avoid a knot of people who had clearly just come from the theater. Was she so close to Covent Garden? No, that couldn't be right. She was supposed to be on Queen Victoria Street, away from the bank. What street was this, exactly?

Along with keeping track of the thoroughfare and unpredictable human bodies in her path, she now peered into the cone of dim light provided by the head-lamps, seeking a street sign. How careless of the city fathers not to provide them. Etching the name of a street into the corner of a building did not help at all in the dark. Ahead, bright lights shone onto the sidewalk, and she heard the subterranean screech of a train.

A station. That would tell her where she was. In moments, she had come abreast of the station's front.

Aldgate. Aldgate Station? That couldn't be right. Why, that would mean she was blissfully driving down *Whitechapel Street* in the middle of the night. She was not on Queen Victoria Street at all!

Oh dear. She had to turn around and get out of here.

Claire steered to the far side of the street and pushed the steering lever all the way out. At the apex of the turn her front tire bumped up onto the sidewalk in front of the station, but there was no help for it. She couldn't reverse unless she got out and pushed, and she was not getting out of this vehicle for all the tea in China. Not in Whitechapel, for the love of God.

Careful. Carefully now. The last thing you want is to dislodge the arrangement of the boiler when you bump back down onto the street. One wheel. Good. Now the oth—

With a communal howl of triumph, a crowd of black shapes pelted out of the mouth of the Underground station and surrounded the landau.

"Lookit this beauty, Snouts! We got a pretty 'un this time, ent we?"

"And a pretty lady to boot. Whatsa matter, lady, want some help unsticking your carriage?"

"No, thank you," Claire said as loudly as her desert-dry throat would allow. "Stand out of the way, please."

"Stand aht the way, please," mimicked a high voice. "Am I in your way, lady? Wot'll you give me and my mates to get aht the way?"

"I shall give you a penny. But you must move first."

"Wot else you got, lady? I bet there's more'n a penny in this pretty carriage."

"Don't touch that!"

"Lady, I wouldn' say you was in a position to be dishin' orders," said a tall, thin shape with an enormous nose. "Give us what you got and then we'll think about movin'."

"Yeah! What'cha got, lady? Bet there's plenty for me in here, eh?"

"Don't open that! Don't, I tell you—it's boiling—"

Too late. The thug had popped open the landau's side hood panel, probably thinking it was a repository for riches, and a cloud of steam billowed out of the boiler. With a scream, he fell back, writhing on the ground clutching his burned face with equally burned hands.

"You bloody rich witch!" screamed someone in the back. "You've hurt Jake!"

With a roar of fury, the entire pack descended on her. Claire just had time to feel her coat ripped from her shoulders when something hard whacked her on the side of the head, and the night whirled around her before she landed hard on the ground.

14

Something dug mercilessly into her ribs. With a groan, Claire cracked open her left eye, and then her right. Her head spun with dizziness and confusion, but she had not been rendered unconscious. At least, she didn't think so. Under her cheek, dirt grated between her skin and the hard cobblestones, stinking of soot, alcohol, and ancient urine. Revolted, she lifted her head.

Something poked her in the ribs again. Blindly, she whipped her arm backward, connecting with empty air. "God help me." It seemed to take an eternity to pull her knees under her, and even longer to get her hands on either side of them.

Her gloves were gone. Bare skin scraped the stones.

She raised her head. The landau. Her trunk. All her worldly goods. Memory rushed in—the shouting, the ridicule, being hit. Falling.

The landau.

The street stood empty, the lamps outside the Aldgate station shining steadily, as though nothing out of the ordinary had happened. Something glinted on the cobbles, and she bent to pick it up, groaning again as the blood rushed to her head.

One of her tortoiseshell hair combs. A tine had snapped off, leaving a gap like the smile of a child without a front tooth. Absently, she reached up and slid it into her chignon. So they had found her traveling case. It seemed too much to hope that they would miss the false bottom in it—at any rate, it had disappeared into the night with them and she was unlikely to see her pearls or her great-grandmother's emerald ring again. At least they had not stolen the very pins from her hair, or the clothes off her body. Her coat, however, with its lovely twining soutache trim, was gone.

The landau. Oh woe. The landau. Tears welled into her eyes as she surveyed the empty, silent street, and scalded a hot track down one cheek.

Something poked the back of her knee.

"Get away!" She whirled, expecting to see a dog nosing at her to see if she was edible, and found instead a child. "Good heavens. Who are you?"

Dressed in a ragged homespun jacket and pants, and a shirt with a fraying band and no collar, the waif turned huge dark eyes on her and pointed into the mouth of an alley across the street. He took a handful of her blue merino skirt—streaked now with something she didn't want to investigate closely—and tugged.

"Oh no, my dear. I know your tricks. If you're hiding another band of miscreants in there, they'll not have me to work over again."

Brave words to a scrap who couldn't be above four years of age. She was as weak as a day-old chick and wouldn't even be able to fight off this child if he decided to do more than poke her.

He shook his head and tugged again on her skirt.

"I'm not going with you, poppet. I must find a bobby and report Mr. Snouts and his friends to the authorities at once."

The ragged head, which might have sported curls if it had been brushed, shook more vigorously. He tightened his grip on her skirt and began to tow her across the street, toward the alley.

"Stop, little man. I'm not going in there. I need to find a policeman. Do you understand? Do you speak English?" He nodded, then made a buttoning motion over his lips, still tugging her toward the alley. "You're not permitted to speak?"

Another nod. He frowned when her stumbling steps stopped, then seemed to get an idea. He dug in one pocket and pulled out her other comb, all its tines intact. After handing it to her, he pointed again at the alley.

Comprehension dawned as she rammed the comb into the other side of her chignon. "They've gone this way? The ruffians who stole my landau and my trunk?" His gap-toothed smile lit up his face in the dim glow from the station lamps across the road. "Aha. Then lead on, little man. It would be useful for the bobbies to have a destination for their investigations once I locate it."

Again the vigorous shake of the head, but he set off at a trot, pulling her by the skirt as though she were a horse on a leading rein. Claire followed him down the empty alley, dodging crates and kegs and even a sleeping human form, its legs sticking out from behind a rubbish bin. The alley doglegged past the door of a tavern, where they both picked up their pace, and disgorged them into a street lined with warehouses of all shapes, piggybacked onto one another and leaving barely enough room to squeeze between. Beyond their ramshackle outlines, she could hear the suck and pull of the Thames as it gurgled against dock and piling.

Squeezed between two warehouses she saw a squat building that might have been a house once, or maybe a customs shed. Even with the moonlight, it was difficult to tell. Its roof raked upward at a steep angle, and it was so narrow a person could stand on one side, toss a stone, and hit the other. The ragged child tugged her skirt as if to moor her to the spot, and pointed.

"They're here? This is where they've taken my things? What is it, some kind of robbers' hideout?" The boy frowned. Too many questions. She tried again. "They've brought my things here?" He nodded. "Are they friends of yours?" He nodded again.

Here was a puzzle. She squatted next to him in the shadow of the neighboring warehouse. "But my little man, if they're friends of yours, why have you showed me? I've said I'll bring the bobbies down on them. Is it because they've hurt you?"

He shook his head so vigorously his matted hair swung straight out above his ears. He took her hand and pointed to the ramshackle place, smiling in a way that she could only interpret as encouraging.

"You want me to go in there?" Big nod. "By myself?" He thrust out his chest and planted his feet as though he were a captain surveying the quarterdeck. "Well yes, I know you're with me, but you probably couldn't stop them coshing me on the head a second time the moment they caught sight of me. All I want is to get my things back. Do you know where they might have put the landau?"

Confusion wrote itself all over the smooth but filthy features.

"Never mind. I shall find it." She rose, the muscles on her right side—the ones that had unceremoniously met the street as she was pulled from the landau— aching with the effort. "And since I haven't seen a member of Sir Robert Peel's policing force in the last hour, I must conclude I'm on my own."

Claire surveyed the building, which leaned against the warehouse next door like a drunk against his best friend. Rage bubbled just beneath her breastbone. How dared they take the clothes literally off her back? How dared anyone treat her like this? It wasn't enough that a mob had invaded her home and caused her to run for her very life. It wasn't enough that her father had made the poor decisions that had opened her up to this. But this scum—these ruffians—had taken everything she had in the world, everything that would have made it possible for her to make her own way. Without respectable clothes and the landau, she could not convince anyone she was worthy of employment, much less gently bred.

These wretches had stolen her future from her, and by all she held holy, she would not tolerate it. She was finished with apologizing and hiding and running away. It was time to stand up and impose her will on someone else for once in her life.

"I'll be back in an hour," she told the youngster still standing beside her, waiting for her to go skipping into that house to have tea and crumpets with his criminal friends. "And if you would be so kind as to make inquiries as to the whereabouts of my landau and meet me out here, I promise I will not involve you in what I'm about to do."

The child's eyes widened and he released her skirt as if it burned him.

She marched down the street, picked up her skirts, and took to her heels in the alley. The last trains ran at eleven o'clock. If she was lucky, she could steal a ride on one and get to the laboratory at St. Cecelia's and back before an Underground conductor caught her without a ticket.

No one occupied the Underground train carriage but two middle-aged charwomen more interested in their own gossip than in what a young lady was doing unaccompanied on a train in the middle of the night. Claire sidled off at Victoria Station, ticketless but unaccosted, and took a shortcut through Eaton Square to the back gate of St. Cecelia's. The administration fondly thought that their property was secure, but the students knew better.

Claire found the foot- and handholds worn into the wall behind the glossy curtain of ivy and clambered up and over in moments. From there it was a quick dash across the lawn and down the basement steps, where skillful application of a hairpin to the lock made the way plain.

The stairs were as dark as criminal activity required them to be, though Claire kept a firm hold on the rail. The last thing she needed was to miss her footing and tumble to the bottom.

Ah. The Chemistry of the Home laboratory.

She found the jar of lucifers Professor Grünwald kept next to his blotter for the purpose of lighting a forbidden cigar during the lunch hour, and by their light set to work. It took a few moments to dredge up the recipe from the recesses of memory—blast the thieves for taking her notebook!—but within a quarter hour she had four vials stoppered and ready to go. Some day, when she was famous and once again rich, she would make an anonymous donation to the school's pitiful science department and make restitution for what she had removed. But for the moment, necessity was most certainly the mother of invention, and on that principle alone even Professor Grünwald might approve.

After bundling her treasure in a used cardigan and then into a leather book satchel, both abandoned in the Lost and Found, she strapped the satchel to her back and retraced her steps. Half an hour later, she stepped out of the alley mouth opposite the rake-roofed home of the rascals who had stolen her things.

No small boy waited for her. Her lips thinned. Well, if he had not taken her seriously before, he most certainly would now.

Keeping to the shadows, she hurried around the corner of a half-timbered warehouse that might have seen active commerce in King Henry's time and removed the vials from her satchel. Their noxious contents gurgled in her hands once she'd refastened the satchel on her back. Since it and the cardigan were her only possessions, she was loath to leave them lying on the street—and the satchel had the advantage of providing storage while allowing her hands free movement.

Thank goodness she'd put on this navy merino suit this morning. The fog breathing off the river was damp and chill, and droplets were already condensing in her hair. The dark color also allowed her to blend into the shadows as she crept from corner to corner of the building. A rat's entry chewed into a board welcomed the first vial. She smashed it into the floorboards. "That's for my notebook, you miserable wretches." A board missing altogether was a fine entry point for the second. "And that's for my pearl necklace." At the third corner, she could find no way in except for a window, so she tossed it through and heard the satisfying tinkle of glass. "My coat, thank you very much." She ran for the front entry as the first noxious tendrils of smokelike gas began to curl out from beneath the boards.

She wrenched open the front door. "And this—" She threw it with all her might. "—is for my landau!"

Someone yelled as the gas did its work, and then pandemonium broke loose. Claire retreated, smiling in satisfaction, as half a dozen figures staggered out in various stages of undress—or not—good heavens—that creature was wearing her coat! Claire flew across the street and tore it off a very short individual who was trailing its lovely panels in the dirt. He—or she, it was difficult to tell—spun in place, both hands mashed to his eyes as he shrieked in pain. Shrugging on her coat, Claire felt as Queen Elizabeth must have at seeing the first of the fire ships succeed so brilliantly against the Spanish armada. It was almost enough to make a person dance a hornpipe.

But she restrained herself, for there in front of her was one of her pretty embroidered waists, being used as a nightdress over a pair of ragged combinations! She dashed over, grasped the hem of it, and pulled it over the filthy girl's head. Weeping with pain, the child turned to her, instinctively seeking to be comforted, but she hardened her heart and stepped away. Finally, the spindly person with the enormous nose staggered out, his face contorted in misery, carrying the waif who had directed her here. The latter's unhappiness was acute, from the sound of the roars emanating from under the coat covering the lad's head.

"Everyone all right?" Snouts croaked, eyes screwed shut in pain. "Mopsies?"

Two cries answered him. One was the girl Claire had relieved of her waist. An identical copy wrapped itself around the first, and they both burst into fresh tears.

"Jake?"

"I'm gonna die, Snouts. Jus' kill me now, eh?"

Ah. Jake, the unfortunate burn victim. His difficulties were only increasing the longer he retained Claire's acquaintance.

"Tigg?"

"'Ere, to my misfortune," wailed the boy who had been wearing Claire's coat.

"'Oo's got Weepin' Willie?" came another voice, belonging to a boy of about twelve who cowered in the gutter, his ragged jacket over his head.

"I gots 'im," Snouts reported. "Can't you 'ear the racket?"

"What happened? Who's set upon us?"

Claire stepped out of the shadows, even though none of them could see yet. "I have."

Silence fell, broken only by the sobbing of Weepin' Willie and the Mopsies.

"'Oo's that, then?" Snouts tried to crack his eyes open, which only resulted in more agony as the condensed gas on his face dribbled into them. "Wot we done to you?"

"You have attacked me, stolen my possessions, and taken my landau," Claire snapped, her voice ringing into the night. "You will return every piece of my property at once or I'll give you a second dose." There were not enough chemicals in the satchel to make good on it, but she would bet not one tortured individual lying in the street was about to take the risk.

"'Oo are you?" Snouts set the wriggling Willie on his feet and sat abruptly in the gutter, still blinded.

"Never mind who I am. But what I am not is some puling victim willing to be cowed and beaten by the likes of you. I demand the return of my property immediately."

The waif—Willie—ran across the road, bawling, and flung himself against her knees. Nonplussed, she stared down at him for a moment, then sighed. "All right. All right then, little man, let me wipe the capsaicin out of your eyes." She knelt, found her handkerchief still in her sleeve, and wiped his face. He wrapped his arms around her neck and sobbed. "Poor darling, why did you not wait for me? I didn't mean for you to be gassed as well."

"'Ow does she know our Willie?" Tigg's voice was muffled from trying to grind his eye sockets into his knees. "She ent gonna hurt 'im any more, is she?"

Claire raised her chin. "Unlike some in present company, I have no intention of hurting anyone. I simply want my things when you are sufficiently recovered to gather them up."

"'Ow long will that be?" Snouts attempted to open his eyes again, and whimpered behind clenched teeth.

"About thirty minutes, I should say." Then she had an idea. "Willie, would you be so kind as to direct me within? I'm quite capable of repacking my trunk myself."

"You leave our Willie alone." The two Mopsies faced her, using their ragged garments to wipe the tears streaming from their eyes. One of them hauled back and kicked Claire in the shin.

"You wretched little monster!"

Claire dropped Willie on the cobbles and caught the girl by the back of her combies as she spun to escape. It was the work of a moment to turn her over her knee and remind her of Newton's law that every action has an equal and opposite reaction.

"Snouts!" the miscreant screamed, wriggling out of Claire's grip and running for her life. "She whacked me!"

"There's a surprise," he mumbled.

"Shoot her!"

"Wiv what? You fink I've got a pistol in me undershorts?"

"But she whacked me!"

"You won't be kicking her again, then, will ya?"

Fuming, the child stamped her foot and shot Claire an evil look, compounded by swollen eyes and a dirty, tear-streaked face. "You'll be sorry, lady."

"I'm afraid you'll be the sorry one if you try to assault me again," Claire informed her. "Honestly, I've never seen such a badly brought-up child, and that's saying something, considering the past several days."

"I ent been brought up, and you're just mean." The moppet stamped again.

"Don't stamp. It isn't ladylike."

Stamp. *Stamp.*

Claire dodged behind Snouts's balled-up form and snatched the disgusting creature by the back of her combies a second time. Again the laws of physics were soundly applied, to the accompaniment of such screeching Claire fully expected either bobbies or criminals to descend on them all like the wrath of God.

She set the child on its feet and silently dared it to stamp again. Its leg twitched once before discretion became the better part. "A wise decision," she told it.

"I'm encouraged to see that you have some capacity for education."

The moppet blinked and ran away to its sister, who put her arms around it and administered what comfort she could to wounded pride and hinder parts.

Claire straightened her spine and surveyed the field of battle. Satisfied that no one had the spirit or the physical capacity to challenge her victory, she held out her hand to Willie. "Would you be so kind as to escort me inside, Master Willie?"

The boy shot an uncertain glance at Snouts.

The latter had at last managed to open one eye just a crack. He waved a defeated hand. "Don't look at me. I ent gonna argue wiv 'er."

16

Inside the derelict building, the gaseous miasma had already begun to clear, not finding the walls and roof any great impediment to its rise through the atmosphere. But Claire still felt a stinging in her eyes, like an echo of the pain endured by the criminals outside.

Criminals, hmph. They were children. How was it possible that so many children should be parentless and forced to make their own way in the world? It was one thing to be eighteen and possessed of an education. It was quite another to be ten ... or four ... and possessed of nothing at all.

Master Willie, being closer to the ground and less affected by the remnants of the gas, found her a lamp on a hook. Then he towed her over to her trunk, which lay empty on its side next to a cold fireplace that appeared not to have been cleaned since the Queen of Empires had begun her glorious reign.

"Ah. Here's a start. Well done." She righted the trunk and laid her embroidered waist inside. Then, holding the lamp high with one hand and her skirts with the other, she followed Willie carefully up a rickety stair—more of a ladder, really—that creaked alarmingly at their combined weight.

As she collected her various bits of clothing—underthings, blouses, walking skirts, dresses, hats—she saw they had already been sorted into heaps with sundry like items that were not nearly as clean. "Willie, were these going to the ragmen in the morning?" He nodded, his eyes tearing a little at the last remnants of the gas. "It's a lucky thing I acted quickly, then. If I had waited, I should never have seen my clothes again. You wouldn't have observed a small traveling case containing a Bible, would you?"

The little boy glanced to the rear of the apartment, where there was a single plank door. Everywhere else, it appeared the members of this gang were using the piles of rags and clothes as bedding until enough had accumulated to go to the ragman or the stall-keepers in Petticoat Lane. But someone rated the privacy and status of a door, and she had one guess as to who that might be.

"Is that Snouts's room?" Willie nodded. "Since he has given me *carte blanche* to recover my property, I shan't feel too bad about invading his privacy, then."

Willie looked alarmed, and she suspected all the children were under threat of death if they, like Bluebeard's wives, succumbed to the temptation to open the door.

For all his status as leader, Snouts had not much more than his minions, she saw as she stepped cautiously inside. A pile of rags, a pipe, a cage containing rags, and a window with real glass in it was the extent of his worldly goods. The room stank of acid alcohol and offal. Primming her mouth in disgust, Claire rooted through the rag-pile until her hands touched a hard and rectangular shape.

Her traveling case. She carried it over to the lamp and opened it to find only the Bible inside. The lock of hair still lay within, so that was another blessing. But what of the rest? She tipped up the false bottom and peered in, then felt the compartment with her fingers.

Nothing. No notebooks, and certainly no jewelry.

"Willie, have you seen any sign of a book and a notebook for writing in? They were in this case." Again, he shook his head, looking worried. "Never mind. I shall have to conduct an interrogation, that's all. Best to do that while the suspects are still somewhat incapacitated. Will you help me return these things to the trunk, please?"

A muffled sound, like water bubbling in a pipe, came as though in reply. Willie's eyes widened and she glanced in the direction of his gaze. "Is there something alive in there?"

What she had mistaken for a heap of rags inside the cage moved and lifted its head. Two black eyes regarded her with suspicion, and the bubbling sound came again.

"Good heavens. Is that a chicken?" Willie gripped the windowsill and stood on tiptoe to peer into the cage. "Snouts keeps a chicken in his room? Why on earth should he do that?" The little boy gestured with both hands and she understood. "Ah. An inexhaustible source of food. What a pity he doesn't understand that one needs to care for one's birds in order to expect something in return." If she had been angry before, it was nothing to what she felt now. This poor creature, locked in the dark with nothing to eat, expected to produce food until—what? It died?

"Come along, little bird." She picked up the cage. "Willie, you are in charge of lighting us downstairs."

In a few moments she had repacked everything into her trunk, and closed the lid. She was not sure how she was going to move it, and she did not yet know where the landau was, but she could only accomplish one thing at a time.

"Thank you for your assistance, Master Willie. Your help has been invaluable."

For the first time, a smile broke out on his face, and she saw a dimple wink on each side of his mouth. He hugged her knees and she dropped to his level, carefully putting the cage on the floor before she hugged him back. When she tried to rise again, he hung on. "What is it, Willie?"

His grip tightened.

"You don't want me to take the bird? No. You don't want me to go outside again? But I must. It is clear that a few of my possessions are secreted upon the persons of your friends, and I intend to retrieve them."

He shook his head, as if her guess was incorrect, and held her immobile with the force of his affection. "What is it, dear? I don't understand."

He released her and ran to the largest rag-pile, where he busied himself making the hollow in it larger, as if to accommodate a—

"Willie, is it that you want me to stay here?"

Beaming, he nodded, and sat himself in the hollow he had made, patting the space next to him. Unaccountably, her eyes filled with tears.

"But my dear, I must go. I must find a place to lay my head this evening, and then continue my search for employment. I appreciate your help deeply, and someday when I can, I will repay you, but I cannot stay."

The smile faded from his face, and even the pathetic hen in the cage made a sad sound. Compassion warred with practicality. It was one thing to rescue a hen that was probably on its last legs anyway. It was quite another thing to rescue a child—or a number of children. Some things were just beyond her means and ability at the moment. She had never realized the power in a child's tears—especially when this particular child had so little, and she was about to take even that away.

"I'm sorry," she whispered. Grasping the hen's cage, she went outside.

The members of the gang—oh, for heaven's sake, the children—had pulled themselves into a knot on the steps of the rope-maker's establishment opposite. When she appeared, they stirred uneasily. Well, they didn't know she had nothing but a cardigan in her satchel, did they?

"Thanks to Master Willie's assistance, I now have most of my things," she said, taking up a schoolteacher's stance before them. "I now require two books, a parcel of pencils, a ring, and a pearl necklace, and I also require the whereabouts of my landau."

They shifted, making themselves smaller on the steps. Snouts gulped audibly and climbed to his feet, brushing the fronts of his patched trousers. "We—we gots a proposition for you, lady." Then he peered through the gloom. "Izzat my Rosie you got there?"

"If you mean this unfortunate scrap of poultry, then yes. I am in the process of rescuing her."

"But she's mine. How'm I gonna eat?"

"I suspect you'll develop the same skills as your companions, Mr. Snouts. You have starved and degraded this poor creature until it's a wonder she'll give you anything but a sound pecking."

"'E caught 'er in t'market in Poultry Street," Tigg said. "'E were gonna eat 'er but t'Mopsies talked 'im out of it."

The Mopsies glared at her, as if she'd singlehandedly undone all their good work. "You may rest assured no one will eat her whilst she is in my care," she assured them. "Now. My property, if you please."

"Our proposition first," Snouts said.

"Mr. Snouts, you are hardly in a position to bargain. I am the one with the poisonous chemicals."

"McTavish."

"I beg your pardon?"

"My name's McTavish. Snouts is just a handle."

"And a fair one it is," Tigg snickered.

"'At's enough! I'm doing a spot o' business 'ere, can't you see?" He turned back to Claire. "Our proposition is, we give you back yer stuff if you stick aroun' an' teach us 'ow to make them chemicals and such."

Willie crept up behind her and wrapped his arms around her knees. Snouts McTavish nodded. "Willie likes yer, so ye must not be like them toffs wot beat us off their fancy carriages."

Memory flared. It had been the day she'd driven Gorse home from school—the day she'd caused the explosion in the laboratory. "That was you. You stopped my landau in front of Pilkington's Hotel. I gave you all the change I had."

Snouts shrugged. "So those're our terms. For every day you stay wiv us an' teach us summink, we give you back one of your gewgaws."

"And my landau?" For the first time, Snouts lost his bravado. He sucked his upper lip into his teeth. "Mr. McTavish, do you have my landau or do you not?"

"Not," he mumbled.

"You don't? Then where is it?"

"Billy Crumwell an' 'is gang stole 'er off us." He met her eyes, pleading. "We 'ad 'er stashed safe as houses, honest, but they followed us. When we went back wiv a buyer—er, I mean, a friend of ours, yer landau were gone."

Claire fought down a rising explosion of rage at having yet another foe to face. "If I stay and teach you, you will help me get it back?"

"Oh, aye, lady. I wouldn't want it nosed about that Snouts McTavish can't 'ang onto 'is plunder." She glared at him. "Ah, I mean, that someone can take wot don't belong to 'em and get away wiv it. It ent honest."

"The hen remains mine."

"Aye," he said reluctantly.

"None of my property shall go missing again."

He gave his companions a look. "Aye."

If she left now to go to her grand-aunts Beaton, she would never see her notebook, full of years of painstaking experimentation, or her great-grandmother's ring again. And the simple fact was, her aunts did not want her there. They were set like summer mud in their own ways, and barely tolerated anyone under fifty, never mind someone just out of school. Her friends could not help, and her mother was hundreds of miles away. She glanced down at Willie, who was still performing the duties of a ball and chain around her knees. He smiled up at her, and her heart turned over.

At least someone in the wide world cared whether she came or went—whether she had a bed for the night or not. It might be Hobson's choice, but at least it was a choice. "Willie and Rosie shall share the upper room with me. I am afraid propriety dictates you must move your things and sleep with your companions, Mr. McTavish."

"And you get all the eggs?"

"Certainly not. We shall save the eggs and have an enormous fry-up, to be shared by all. That is, provided we find some corn and perhaps some greens for Rosie to eat in the meantime. She is not an automaton. She must be cared for."

"We'll find food for 'er, lady." The Mopsie that Claire had not paddled spoke up. The other one rubbed its behind and remained mutinously silent.

"We are agreed, then. I will teach you how to construct my gaseous capsaicin devices, and you will return my things and assist me in the recovery of my landau."

Snouts nodded, and slowly the others followed his lead.

"Wot's yer name?" the boy who had worn her coat asked. "We can't call yer 'lady 'oo makes the devices' all the time."

Claire hesitated a moment. "Lady will do for now. It has the advantage of being both true and anonymous."

"Wot's nominus?"

"What I choose to be until I make something of myself, that's what. Now, then. I have observed that the gas I released inside, while it made you uncomfortable, had the side benefit of killing all the vermin in the place. Shall we all adjourn and see what comfort we can find in our lodgings?"

17

It cannot be said that Claire spent a comfortable night on her rag-pile. While Willie breathed gently next to her, she started and woke at every sound, suspecting thievery or vermin—she wasn't sure which would be worse. When a watery dawn finally broke over London, she was already awake and regretting the absence of tooth-powder and warm water to wash in.

Clearly, better accommodations must join recovery of her property and employment on her list of immediate needs.

She combed her hair with her uninjured tortoiseshell comb, rewound it and pinned it into its customary chignon. Then she changed into a fresh waist and descended the stair with Rosie in her cage in one hand.

The sound of conversation led her into the depths of the house, where she found her companions, including Willie, gathered in the kitchen around a three-legged table. A stack of bricks replaced the fourth leg.

Kitchen was a generous term. The room contained only a cold iron stove and the table, and the shelving tacked onto the walls above the stove were empty but for dirt and spiders. In the center of the table, a hard loaf had been hacked at with a pocket-knife, and the children were busy wolfing it down.

"Good morning," she greeted them. "Where did this come from?"

A mumble answered her. Rosie tottered to her feet and focused on the bread on the table, tilting her head so as not to lose sight of it.

"We already been out," a Mopsie said. "I got a corncob for Rosie." She extracted it from a pocket and held it up.

"I could've et that," Jake complained. "I'm still hungry." Someone had wrapped a rag around his burned hands.

Claire opened the cage door and put the fresh ear inside. Rosie fell upon it like an eagle on a carcass. "A little self-sacrifice now will all be forgotten when we have our fry-up later in the week. May I have some of that bread, please?"

"Help yerself," Jake said.

"Mr. Jake, a gentleman would slice a piece and offer it to a lady."

"I ent no gentleman."

"Since I am a lady, and since I do not consort with men who are not gentlemen, your training in that department begins immediately." She smiled at him. "Thank you. You are most generous."

He just stared at her.

"Crikey, Jake, you deaf? Cut 'er off a bit." Snouts pushed the knife closer to him.

"I ent servin' 'er. What d'ye take me for?"

"It is not a matter of serving, Mr. Jake. A gentleman puts the comfort of others before his own. That is how one tells he *is* a gentleman."

"I said I weren't a gentleman. Cut yer own bread. Or better yet, don't, and I'll 'ave it."

Snouts swore and cuffed him across the head. "Do as she says, ye stupid cove."

"Why should I? First she burns me, then she boils me eyes. If I take that knife to anything, it'll be 'er, and that's a fact."

Though he couldn't be more than twelve or thirteen, Claire could not mistake the deadly resolve in his eyes and had no doubt he meant exactly what he said. "I did warn you not to raise the landau's front panel, Mr. Jake," she said in quiet but firm tones. "You chose to ignore me. And as for the gaseous capsaicin, we're going to turn that to our advantage and you shan't have to experience it again."

"About that," Snouts said as Jake reluctantly picked up the knife and sawed off a chunk of the dark bread. Claire took it and tried to chew a few bites. Then she tore the remainder into bits and gave them to Rosie, who launched herself at them with enthusiasm.

"Yes, about that. The first thing to do is to compile the ingredients." She told them what she would need. "Are you able to find these things?"

Snouts and Tigg exchanged a glance. "Sure. We'll just stroll into the nearest chemist's or apothecary's and pick those up."

"Lovely." Claire smiled.

"I 'ope you 'ave lots of dosh, lady, because those things don't sound free. Or easily liberated, if you get my drift."

"Dosh?"

"Cash. Blunt. Pounds sterling."

She had no such thing. She had never carried more than a few shillings for sweets, and had no doubt at all that the household money had been looted from wherever Mrs. Morven kept it in Carrick House. "I'm afraid not. What shall we do, then?"

The Mopsies elbowed each other and grinned. Snouts jerked his chin in their direction. "These 'uns 'ave a few useful talents along those lines. At least it ent the Lord's Day. Pickings is always slim in the church crowd."

"Pick—?" And then the penny dropped. "Oh, no. No. You will not be stealing from people's pockets the means to obtain these items. Absolutely not."

Five pairs of eyes turned on her with incredulity. "Beggin' yer pardon, lady, but where d'you suppose the bread and corn came from?"

"I have no idea." Someone had gone to the market, hadn't they?

Snouts shook his head at her ignorance, and Claire began to feel nettled. "Babes in the woods," he sighed. "Rag-pickin' don't cover expenses. If we don't steal, we don't eat, simple as that. If you've strong opinions on't, I suggest we end our association 'ere."

"Not until I get my landau back."

"Then yer goin' t'be awful hungry along about Wednesday."

Sleeping rough was one thing. But descending to criminal activity simply to eat? Unheard of. Unacceptable. As it was, she was walking the knife's edge—if it were discovered where she was, she could never be received again in polite society.

"Good heavens, Mr. McTavish. Has it never occurred to you that there are alternatives to stealing? Such as employment, for instance?"

"'Oo's gonna employ the likes of us?" Tigg wanted to know.

She surveyed the ragged, filthy band. Point taken. "Well, if we cannot earn our bread by the skill of our hands, we must earn it by the power of our intellect. How many of you have your numbers?"

No response.

"None of you can count? Or do arithmetic?"

Silence.

"Dear me. All right. I can see I have my work cut out for me. So let me ask you this—do any of you gentlemen know where the gaming parlors are?" At this, every male hand but Willie's went up. "Ah. I thought as much. Are we possessed of a pack of cards?"

Tigg reached over and removed the lid of the stove. He rummaged inside and withdrew a pack of dog-eared and dirty cards, tied into a bundle with a piece of hemp. "Keeps 'em dry in there," he said by way of explanation. "What does knowing our numbers 'ave to do with the gaming parlors, lady?"

"Simply this. Unless one knows the values of the numbers, one cannot play cards successfully. And unless one plays successfully, one cannot win the pot. Do you see my reasoning now?"

Their eyes widened as the bright vista of possibility opened up to them. "Gather round, all of you. I'm going to teach you your numbers—yes, even you, Willie— and then I'm going to teach you a game of skill and strategy. To the inhabitants of the Wild West, it's known as cowboy poker."

18

Andrew Malvern had not known that James, always so hearty and hail-fellow-well-met, was a proud man. But it was quite plain that he possessed that vice, and that Lady Claire Trevelyan had injured it, whether she'd meant to or not. The fact that his partner struggled with a vice he did not didn't bother him. After all, Andrew himself struggled with his temper and a tendency to fall into a glass of whiskey when he was tired and frustrated.

No, what bothered him was that because James considered himself snubbed by the young lady, he, Andrew, had lost the possibility of a fine assistant. How many gently bred young ladies, after all, were not only possessed of a landau and the skill to pilot it, but read scientific journals to boot? It galled him, frankly, and he was quite put out with his friend even now.

In fact, he was so put out that he couldn't stay in his own laboratory, for fear that James would return and he would say more things he couldn't take back. Instead of sending a tube to place another order of coal and chemicals, he had gone to the coal-yard himself, and then to the manufactory. He'd taken his evening meal with a glass of foamy beer at his mother's cottage in Stratford, and watched the sun set over the smoke of London feeling full but not content.

He heard the whisper of her skirts upon the terrace a moment before she joined him. "It's been a while since I've seen you and young Lord James on the outs, Andrew. Why don't you tell me about it?"

"There is nothing you can do, Mother."

"I can listen. It's clear you need to get it off your chest, and you know it'll go no further."

That was true. A former lady's maid, his mother had married a policeman who had advanced through the ranks to captain of his own detachment before he'd passed on. As confidante to both, she was the repository of secrets that even he was not permitted to know—such as what really caused the Duchess of Tavistock to divorce her husband, or what might have happened to the infant Lord Wilberforce Dunsmuir, who had disappeared two years ago from his bed under the very nose of his nurse. His mother had been employed in both households in her youth and in the latter case, still kept in contact with the nurse, sending the poor woman a basket of food every now and then to keep her from starvation.

"Very well." He told her the whole story and ended with, "So there you have it. A woman's come between us at last—but not in the way I might have expected."

"The poor child," his mother murmured. "Viscount St. Ives's daughter, you say?"

"The very same. Now reduced to earning her bread like the rest of us—though I must say she doesn't behave like your average Blood. She plans to put herself through university."

"It will take more than the wages you can give her to do that."

"I know, but I admire her for her ambition, at least. And there are scholarships to be had."

"If one has the right connections."

"Wit or Blood, I'm sure she does."

His mother reached across the glass table for the newspaper that sat folded there. "I thought her name sounded familiar. Did you see this?" She opened the *Evening Standard* to the front page.

RIOT IN BELGRAVIA LEAVES BURNING QUESTIONS

Last evening the titled residents of Belgravia were treated to a shocking example of unbridled brigandry that prompted butlers up and down the tidy streets to lock doors and seek out the nearest fireplace poker. Carrick House was the focus of a mob of fifty or more, all of whom were whipped into an emotional frenzy by a speaker at Hyde Park Corner. The crowd adjourned to Wilton Crescent, where they converged upon the house of the late Viscount St. Ives, whom many are accusing of being the engineer behind the infamous Arabian

Bubble. Whether this is true or not, the crowd obviously believed it to be so. With windows broken and furniture
burned, this reporter was shocked to the core at such a public
display of bad feeling.

A bystander said the uncontrollable mob was shouting about
recouping its investments. "But that's hardly reasonable
when they made a bonfire in the street out of items they
could have sold," he said. "I feared for the lives of the remaining occupants of the house."

Indeed, according to reports, the sister of the present viscount
was believed to have been in residence at the time, along
with one or two loyal retainers. Her whereabouts at present
are not known.

"Great Scott." Andrew held the paper up. "It says
no one knows where she is."

"So now I ask myself, is this tiff really over the
young lady and Lord James, or the young lady and
you, my dear boy?"

Andrew put the paper down and rose. "She is a
young woman of intellect and spirit, Mother. This is
not about a tiff at all—anyone would be concerned for
a person of their acquaintance."

"Certainly," she agreed.

"Any gentleman with an ounce of humanity would
be shocked at such a report."

"Of course."

"I shall take my leave now, Mother. Thank you for
supper."

"My compliments to Lord James when you make it
up with him. And to the young lady when you find
her."

He paused in the act of putting on his bowler. "Mother."

She made a gesture as though she were buttoning her lips, and smiled as she kissed him goodbye.

He caught an evening train into Victoria Station and walked the few blocks into Belgrave Square at a fast clip. The smell of burned, wet wood hung on the air as he rounded the corner into Wilton Crescent, and though he had never been to Carrick House, it wasn't difficult to tell which had been Lady Claire's home.

It was the only one on the crescent with no windows left on the ground floor. The white-painted Georgian exterior was smudged with black handprints, and the sidewalk in front had been trampled to the point that bricks had come loose, like teeth after a blow.

Dismayed, he stared from the house to the street, where dustmen were still loading the last charred and broken pieces of furniture into their wagon. One of them saw his face and paused to direct a stream of chewing tobacco into the still-smoking heap.

"Shame, innit?" he said affably.

"That it is." Understatement of the year.

"Eejits, all of 'em. Her ladyship'll not be able to get half the dosh she might've before. If they're lookin' for their money back, they just done themselves out of a bundle of it."

"I daresay you are right." Andrew scanned the house once more. "Her ladyship is not in residence?"

"Not that I know. Was supposed to be a daughter still 'ere but there's been no sign of 'er, and I been 'ere since teatime. Prob'ly be an hour or so more, once t'lamps come on."

Andrew dug in his breast pocket. "If you see her, could you give her my card?"

The dustman peered at it in the gloom. "Wot're you, some sort of solicitor or summink?"

"No, just a—" Well, what was he, exactly? "A friend. A very concerned friend. I should like to know she's safe, at the very least."

"Can't fault a man fer that." The dustman pocketed the card. "S'a shame."

It was as good an epitaph as any. Andrew thanked the man and began his walk back to Victoria Station. He had inherited his father's aptitude for puzzles, and here was one that involved not only the brain, but also the sympathies of a gentleman. Lady Claire's incursion into his life had been brief but brilliant, and he could not now walk away. He must apply his mind to finding her himself.

19

As it turned out, Snouts possessed the greatest aptitude, not for numbers, but for bluffing. "It is that talent that will allow you to win," Claire assured him.
"Such a skill cannot be taught. In the meantime, let us
count these diamonds once more—if you have three on
this card and four on this one, how many do you have
in total?"

Tigg and Jake had at one time in their dark pasts
received some schooling, so addition and subtraction
came back fairly quickly. The Mopsies, however,
treated the concept of multiplication with dark suspicion. To them, it was simply not possible to arrive at a
single answer in a multitude of ways. One added three
to three to get six, one did not simply say, "twice

three" and arrive at six. Since there were only four suits, Claire could only advance to the four times table in any case. Everything after that would have to be memorized ... another day.

Without slates, chalk, or books, they were limited to what the cards could teach them, and as the day tilted into afternoon, she and Snouts needed the deck themselves. They played hand after hand of poker until Tigg nudged her.

"We can't do this much longer, lady. Everyone'll be stumblin' off 'ome soon to get a bit of shut-eye before tonight's games."

"We want to play when they're tired and foxed." Snouts gathered up the cards and tapped them into a neat deck. "Only one problem I see."

"What would that be?" Claire lifted the stove lid so he could put the cards back in their place. "You have all done very well today. Even Jake can play a respectable hand, though I would not bet the deed to an estate on it."

"That's just it," Snouts said. "What 'ave we got to bet wiv besides great lots of nuffink?"

Claire sat rather suddenly on the broken stool she had been using. "Oh. I had not got that far in my strategy." She regarded him while her mind raced and anxiety puddled in her stomach. How could she not have thought of this? The whole point of gambling was to win, but one had to have a stake in order to be included in the game.

She did not even have a toothpick.

But wait—

Her gaze narrowed on Snouts. "We do have something to throw in the pot," she said. "Where is my exchange for teaching you your numbers? Where is my great-grandmother's ring?"

"You get yer stuff back when you teach us about chemicals and suchlike useful items." Jake tilted his chair back, severely endangering its bodily integrity. "Not arithmetic."

"Shut up, Jake." Snouts reached under the muffler wound about his neck and rummaged in his shirt. "This it?"

Her great-grandmother's Georgian emerald winked in his palm. Claire restrained herself from snatching it by sitting on her hands. She would not say she had gained their trust, but at least she was making every effort she could to help them in their uneasy truce. However, it seemed she would have to make this ultimate sacrifice in order to attain the greater goal.

"Yes, that's it." With a breath, she committed herself. "We will use it for our stake. I implore you to use your skills to the utmost, Mr. McTavish. I should very much like to see it come back again."

"I ent goin' into this wiv the intent to lose it, if that's wot you mean." He tucked the ring away.

"I still say we pawn the thing," Jake put in. "Stupid to risk it when we could get ten pound easy over t' Seven Dials."

"We ent goin' to pawn the lady's ring if we have a chance of winnin' the pot," Tigg told him.

"What chance? Snouts ent no strategy man. You've got me for that."

"But you cannot recognize the numbers on the cards fast enough," Claire reminded him. "Snouts is our best chance."

"I c'n tot them up pretty quick," one of the Mopsies said with pride. "Faster'n you, Jake."

In answer, he swatted her with the back of his bandaged hand. In the resulting uproar, Snouts grabbed him and pushed him out into the front room. "I've 'ad about enough of you!" he shouted. "Go do summat useful and don't lemme see you back 'ere afore dark." Jake's broken boots pounded furiously on the street, disappearing into the hubbub dockside. "Stupid cove." Snouts went to the back door and looked out, though there was nothing there but tangled weeds and broken rocks, and the river wall six feet away.

Claire opened Rosie's cage and took her out, sliding one hand under her feet and passing her arm about her so she would not fall off. Rosie settled onto her hand, and Claire felt her feet relax.

Ah. She had gained the hen's trust. Now she would not run away to become food for who knew what kind of four- or two-legged predator. She deposited the bird gently on the ground outside, where Rosie immediately began divesting the property of its insect life.

"She'll run off," Snouts said.

"She will not. We have fed her, you see, and provided a hunting ground. She has no reason to run. Mr. McTavish, would you have pawned the ring this morning if we had not decided to use it?"

"Aye."

"Thank you for not doing so. At least this way we have a chance of getting it back."

"Means summat to ya, does it?"

"It was my great-grandmother's. The emerald came from the crown of an Indian prince. Or so family legend has it, at least. I should hate to lose something that has come so far and been with us so long."

Rosie pounced on a beetle with energy.

"I'll do me best," Snouts said, his voice gruff as he watched the bird. "Ent often a lady trusts me with 'er family hairlooms."

Claire smiled at him. "Good luck, Mr. McTavish. You'd best be off now."

"What'll you do?"

"I shall run the Mopsies through their four times tables once again, and then I must find a way to let my friends know I have not been kidnapped or pushed into the river."

"You won't tell 'em of us? Or cut an' run?"

"Of course not. We have an agreement, and it is not yet fulfilled. I shall be here when you return triumphant, you may depend upon it."

She had gained Rosie's trust with a cob of corn and some bread. It would take a prince's emerald to gain the trust of Snouts McTavish and his gang. But it was a price she was willing to pay if it meant getting her life back again. What shape that life would take was a mystery at the moment. But surely the good Lord could not expect her to waste the talents He had given her by going meekly down to Cornwall to become the wife of some husky lad whose idea of literature was the local cattle prices.

"I'm 'ungry," one of the Mopsies announced. "We'll be back."

And before Claire could grab them and remind them that stealing was a crime, she and Tigg had vanished out the front. The remaining Mopsie sat upon the river wall and glared from her to Rosie in a way that told Claire exactly where her suspicions lay.

"I meant what I said, you know," Claire informed the child. "No harm shall come to Rosie whilst she is in my care. She has given me her trust, so she will not run away. Nor do you need to stand guard over her."

The child blinked at her. "Wot's 'at?"

"Say, 'I beg your pardon'."

"I beg yer pardon, wot's 'at?"

Claire sighed. "Once a bird gives you her trust, she regards you as a member of her flock. If I were you, I should endeavor to gain Rosie's trust as well. One cannot have too many members in one's flock."

"I brought 'er a corn even when Jake would've et it."

"Next time you shall give it to her from your own hand, so that she realizes you are also worthy of her trust."

The child eyed her. "Yer a strange mort."

"Why should you say that?"

"Most people just eat chickens and don't care wot they fink."

"Yes, well, no one is eating Rosie. She has a duty to perform and we shall enable her to do it. Just as you do. What is twice three?"

"I dunno."

"Yes, you do. If I have three cobs of corn and you have three cobs, how many do we have to give to Rosie altogether?"

The wheels ground into motion. "Six. But she'd be sick for sure if she et 'em all at oncet."

"She would indeed. However, if she ate only one, how many would be left?"

"Five."

"One for each day of the week. A very satisfactory arrangement for Rosie, I should say, wouldn't you?"

"If Snouts wins 'at poker game, we could 'ave 'em."

"Let us hope he does, then. Would you do me the honor of telling me your name?"

The child gazed at her sideways while she studied Rosie, who had found a patch of bare dirt and was busy digging a dust bath. "I'm a Mopsie."

"But you must have a Christian name."

"I dunno."

"You don't know your name?" Here was a sad situation. Chickens were worthy of names but little girls with sticky fingers were not?

"I gots a name, I just dunno as I should tell you. Snouts said not if the coppers was to ask."

"I am not a copper. And if we are to be members of Rosie's flock, it is only fitting that we address each other correctly."

She mulled this over. "I'm Maggie. Short for Margaret, but 'at takes too long to say."

Claire leaned over and offered her hand, and bemused, Maggie shook it. "A pleasure, Miss Maggie. And your sister?"

"She's Lizzie. Elizabeth."

With a smile, Claire said, "My middle name is Elizabeth. I was named for my grandmother, who was reckoned a great beauty in her day. My mother, as you see, was an optimist."

"Lizzie's a beauty," Maggie said defensively, as if her sister was not to be outdone by any other Elizabeth in the country, alive or not.

"She is indeed. She has very striking blue eyes. I hope she has forgiven me for spanking her last night."

"Nope."

"She did kick me first, and may I say, it was completely unwarranted. I hope her heart may soften toward me in time, if we are to be flock mates as well."

Maggie fell silent, watching Rosie fling dirt over herself with great abandon. Then she said, "Why's she making 'erself all dirty?"

"She is having a bath. The dirt suffocates any bugs, and leaves her feeling shiny and clean when she shakes it out."

"'Ow's a fine lady like you know so much about hens, then?"

"Polgarth the poultryman taught me when I was as old as you. He was wise in the ways of birds. We have the finest flock in the parish, and every bird in it trusts him with her life."

"They're flock mates, then."

"They are indeed."

Maggie glanced at her. "Jake don't trust you. Ent he a flock mate?"

Claire hesitated. "In some cases it takes time. And I don't think offering a corn cob to him is going to do the trick."

To her surprise, Maggie smiled widely, dimples winking in her dirty cheeks. "'E likes corn. Try it."

Claire smiled too, more at the unexpected companionship in the child's gap-toothed grin than at the image of Jake taking anything from her otherwise than by force or stealth. "I think the price of his trust is substantially higher than corn. I'd have to offer him my pearl necklace at the least."

"'Ere, then." Maggie reached under her combinations and pulled out the double strand of St. Ives pearls. Claire stared at them, pale against the girl's grubby hand.

"Take 'em." Maggie tossed them over, and Claire caught them more by reflex than aim.

"I don't understand. I haven't shown you any chemical formulas yet."

"Jake'd just take 'em in the night and pawn 'em if he knew I had 'em. That's why Snouts didn't tell 'im. But we're flock mates, and Jake's afraid of you."

Claire hardly knew which astonishing fact to address first. "Tha—thank you, Maggie. It's very … commendable of you to return them unasked." She fastened them round her neck and pushed them beneath the collar of her blouse. "Jake does not strike me as being afraid of anyone."

"'E's afraid of you. He talks a hard streak, but I know. Otherwise he'd've knifed you straight out."

"Would he?" Claire sat down rather suddenly on the filthy back step. "I must consider myself fortunate, then." Perhaps it would be best to change the subject. "I must go and send a tube," she said. "Mr. McTavish will not be back for some time yet. Would you like to come with me?"

Maggie shook her head. "Rosie and me will stay behind." Rosie shook out her feathers in a cloud of dust and stalked over to recline upon the ground next to Claire's dusty kid half-boots.

"You might take the opportunity to clean her cage and find some fresh bedding, then," Claire suggested. "Since she has performed her ablutions, she may wish to lay an egg."

At the prospect of the imminent arrival of food, Maggie hopped off the wall and went to get the cage. Upon the ground, Rosie blinked in slow contentment. One creature, at least, was perfectly happy in this moment. Claire went in and put on her hat and blue merino jacket, wished fruitlessly for a mirror, and set off.

20

She had never realized with such painful clarity how much she had taken even a shilling for granted. Without such a simple thing, she could not in good conscience take the Underground again to Victoria Station. She could not pay to have a tube sent from the Post Office, so she was forced to consider returning home. But Belgravia was a long walk from the docks.

Claire set her teeth. Snouts would return victorious. They would get the ingredients they needed for the gaseous devices. They would retrieve the landau tonight, and she would not have to walk anywhere henceforth. But in the meantime, she had miles to go, she was ravenously hungry, and her strictures against stealing were beginning to seem foolish.

No wonder Maggie wanted to stay behind to ensure the safety of the egg.

Claire felt dangerously out of place as she pushed and dodged her way along the streets. The markets might be closing up for the day, but the desperate crowds jostled her, men looked at her askance, and bands of thin, ragged children tugged at her skirts, begging. Little did they know she was as penniless and homeless as they. In fact, the only difference between them was that she possessed an education and a clean waist, and they did not. Her boot heel slipped in a mash of rotten fruit, and she fetched up against the side of a cart, whose owner shouted at her. Blushing, furious at her circumstances, she stumbled away and hurried up the street as fast as she was able, clutching her hat.

Half an hour's sweating walk brought her back to the Embankment, and the sweep of another hour saw her at last in the quieter confines of Mayfair, where at least the air she breathed was free of stink and the invective of angry stall-keepers. Of course, she looked as though she had been dragged through a row of market stalls willy-nilly. Her skirt was stained in two places, her half-boots were filthy, and her navy straw hat had been knocked askew so many times she was sure her hair looked like a mares' nest.

Wilton Crescent. *Thank you, Lord.* If only she could reach—

She stopped on the pavement as though she had run into a sheet of glass.

Broken windows. Charred walls. In the middle of the street, a huge black smear littered with coals of burned wood told her that Peony had been chillingly correct in her predictions. But what of Gorse and Mrs. Morven? Where had they gone? And was there anything left within?

She picked her way up the sidewalk. There was no hope of restoring the herringbone pattern of the brick—it had been crushed and broken beyond repair. The front door swung open with a creak that told her it had withstood severe strain, but would never lock again. The front hall was utterly empty. The drawing room a shambles—the velvet drapes pulled down and stolen, their rings kicked into the corners, all the furniture gone. The music room ... Claire gulped and steeled herself. Her harp had gone down to Cornwall on the dray, so at least she would not have the heartbreak of looking at its ruin. Then she blinked. The piano was still here. She touched a key. Its weight must have defeated the mob—and they must have forgotten to bring axes along to demolish it inside. But it stood in a room that was empty save for the broken glass on the parquet floor.

"Mrs. Morven?" she called on the stairs to the kitchen. "Gorse? Are you here?" Silence answered her— the most profound she had ever heard in the house.

The kitchen had, of course, been looted of everything Mrs. Morven had so carefully inventoried. A few pots remained, sundry bits of cutlery, even a basket. But she had to admit this was more than they had in her current bolt-hole, where the sole cooking implements were a spirit lamp, a cast-iron frying-pan, and a dented copper pot, all lifted from various refuse heaps after having been tossed as unusable.

An idea whisked through her brain like a rat disturbed in a dark room. This was still her home—and even in its broken state it was better shelter than the slant-roofed squat. Could she bring Snouts and his gang here until the terms of her bargain were fulfilled?

She climbed the stairs, noting that several of the oak spindles in the banister had been kicked out, likely to serve as kindling for the bonfire outside. The bedrooms had been looted, too, and most of the linens carried away. But for a miracle, the mattress remained on her bed, askew in its mahogany frame. The combination of the four-poster's weight and the pitch of the staircase had probably saved it. And look, the linens in the closet, set discreetly inside the wall, were still here. But the books had been tumbled from the bookcase and scattered from one end of the third floor to the other. Half of them appeared to have been used for kindling as well.

With a sigh, her heart like a boat-anchor in her chest, she proceeded to the fourth floor. For a miracle, nothing seemed to have been broken or even disturbed. They had not reached this far. A busy buzzing sound caught her attention, and she pushed open the door to what had been Silvie's room. The last mother's helper paddled busily at the dhurrie as though nothing were amiss.

Claire sat suddenly on a ladder-back chair while the tears welled uncontrollably in her eyes. The mother's helper was almost the only thing remaining from her old life. To see it going about its business as though Silvie would come running in at any moment to fetch some skin salve for Lady St. Ives was so ridiculous and comical and pathetic that Claire could not help it.

"What am I going to do?" she asked it when the paroxysm of grief had passed. Her chest jerking with a dry sob, she palmed the tears from her cheeks like a child. "What will become of us all?"

The mother's helper bumped against the iron leg of the bedstead, turned left, and buzzed beneath it, intent upon its duty. It had no answers for her. She must come up with them herself.

First things first. Was there still a sheet of paper in the house? And a tube?

The answer to the first was no. Not one, unless she counted the end-papers of the books on the floor. But three tubes waited in the vacuum chamber, thank goodness. The first was a letter from the butler at Wellesley House, welcoming Gorse to the staff and stating that his duties would begin on the twenty-first of June.

Claire had lost track of her life so thoroughly that she could not for the life of her think what the date might be. She opened the next tube. A bill from Madame du Barry for her evening dresses. With a snort, she laid it aside. The back would do nicely for her purposes, and the good lady was going to have to sing for her dresses. The third tube contained a single card with—how very strange—Andrew Malvern's name and address on the front. She turned it over. The word *concerned* was written on the back in what appeared to be charcoal in an almost unintelligible scrawl. She had seen Mr. Malvern's square, legible hand on some of the documents on his desk, and unless he had deteriorated substantially in the last several days, this was not his writing.

Singular. And puzzling. *Concerned.* Hm. She was no concern of his. He would do better to turn his energies to his choice of business partner.

She slipped the card into her glove and began searching the kitchen. At length, rammed at the back of a drawer, she found a stub of pencil. Her mother would find it an even greater puzzle to receive a letter written on the back of a bill, but desperate times required desperate measures, and the escritoire was probably in Exeter by now.

Dear Mama,

I hope this finds you and my brother well. You should be seeing the arrival of the dray with the small items of furniture and plate shortly. It left Saturday. We are having a little difficulty selling Carrick House but I expect Mr. Arundel will continue to do his best.

I have taken a position as governess to six children, ranging in age from fourteen to four, including twin girls. They have no shortage of intelligence and we are presently engaged in learning our numbers. For this reason I will not be joining you and my brother for some few weeks.

My position is not permanent, but it is necessary at present.

Your loving daughter,
Claire

She spun the letters and numbers on the tube to form the code for Gwynn Place, and watched the vacuum system suck it away to the Victoria switching station, where it would begin the series of relays down to Cornwall. So, for at least a few weeks, her mother would believe her to be safe and would be unlikely to dispatch a bobby to escort her to Victoria Station and ensure that she boarded the Dutchman.

Claire climbed the stairs and found an endpaper lying on the hall runner that would do nicely for Emilie.

My dear friend,

I am sorry I could not stay to converse with you last night, but twilight was falling and I needed to reach my aunts Beaton without delay. You will be happy to know I have taken a position as a governess. It offers more independence than I expected and I am presently engaged in the study of mathematics with my six charges.

I will be much occupied over the next several weeks but I beg you not to worry.

Your affectionate
Claire

With a hiss, the second missive began its much briefer journey over to Cadogan Square. Claire could only hope that Emilie was in the habit of intercepting her own mail, otherwise she would have sacrificed an end-paper to the Fragonard drawing-room fire. She returned to the third floor and began to collect end-papers and frontispieces from the shards of books on the floor. If Tigg and the others were to advance beyond the four times table, she would need something to write on. She tucked them in her satchel and surveyed the bedrooms. What else? Linens? No. There were no beds to put them on. Basin and ewer? Smashed. Clothes? She was hard put to carry the trunk she had. No point in bringing anything else along.

The painful truth was, she could not bring anything from her old life with her. Nor could she bring Snouts and the others here, sensible though that idea was. They could not be coming and going in Mayfair without danger of arrest simply for being where they were. It was up to her to resign herself to living rough until she had done what she had promised to do.

But in the meantime, life could be made a little easier, could it not? Back on the fourth floor, in Mrs. Morven's room, she found a spare packet of tooth powder and a bar of soap. The good lady would not begrudge them, and Claire would reimburse her as soon as she could. She scooped up the mother's helper and it immediately stopped moving. Tucking it under her arm, she descended the stairs.

Where was Mrs. Morven? And Gorse?

She had no way to tell them she was safe, and no way to find out if they were. All she could do was leave a note in their shambles of a kitchen and hope that one of them would return and find it. She wrote something brief and cheerful on an end-paper and left it on the chopping block. Then she picked up half a dozen metal forks and two slightly bent knives from the floor and tucked them in her satchel, with the mother's helper going into the basket. If there was to be food today, at least they would have the wherewithal to eat it.

Food. Her stomach must surely be sticking to her backbone. In this house of plenty, could she not at least find something to keep body and soul together? At the very back of the cold cupboard, she found an apple, aged and wrinkled. With relief and a sense that she was behaving very much like poor Rosie, she devoured it in seconds. It did not fill her stomach, but at least she could face the long walk back to the squat with something approaching fortitude.

The squat. Another night lying on the rag-pile. And the prospect of Jake, who would have knifed her if his fear hadn't overridden his hatred.

Outside on the step, she ran a gentle hand over the panels of the door as it did its best to close. For a moment, she leaned against it, eyes closed, breathing in the smell of paint and slightly splintered wood. Then she turned her face to the street and steeled herself to leave home once again.

21

"Twenty quid! *Twenty quid!*" Snouts riffled the ragged pile of bills in Claire's face and danced a jig around her. "I'm the king of cowboy poker and I'm rich!"

With a laugh, Claire watched him attempt to polka with Tigg, who pushed him off with a "Garn, ya big lummox!" Then she folded her arms. "You mean to say, of course, that *we* are rich. Since this was a community effort, we all share in the spoils."

"Ah ... but it was me puttin' me 'ead in the lion's mouth, as it were."

"Nonsense. The lions were drunk as lords and too bleary-eyed to see. It was a case of superior apprehension of strategy on your part, timing on Tigg's part, and a lavish stake on my part. Which I would like returned, if you please."

Whatever else he might be, she had observed that Snouts was a practical boy. Not only was he outnumbered, but the outnumbering parties were hungry, anxious, and not too proud to take him to the ground if he gave her any more guff. He dug about his person and produced the emerald ring. Claire's fingers closed around it with an internal prayer of thanks. Then she slipped it on the middle finger of her right hand—the only one it fit—and held out her left hand, palm up.

Snouts eyed her. "Now, lady, even you will say it's fair for me to 'ave me winnings once you've got your property back."

"I'm grateful to have my stake returned. But as I've said, the winnings belong to all. We must save five pounds to stake the next game. Each member here receives two, to spend as they wish. That leaves five pounds for you, Mr. McTavish, which you must admit is far more than you would otherwise have had without our help."

"An' what about them chemicals?" Jake wanted to know.

"You are quite correct, Mr. Jake. I can obtain the chemicals with one of my two pounds. With the other, I must have something to eat or I shall fall down where I stand. We do not even have a loaf of bread this morning. Who's with me?"

Maggie and Willie crowded her skirts. "Can we 'ave a sweet?"

She looked down into two pairs of eyes, both shadowed with dirt and more care than a child should ever be burdened with. "I should think that a sweet would be a fitting reward for a job well done in the field of mathematics. And we must not forget Rosie while we are enjoying the fruits of our labors."

"She laid an egg," Maggie said in a confidential tone. "I hid it."

Lizzie hung back, her face cloudy as the desire to go fought with the necessity of its being in Claire's company.

"Miss Elizabeth, we would be glad of your company if you should care to join us."

"My name's Lizzie."

"Of course it is—to your family. But it would be impertinent of me to address you so familiarly on such short acquaintance."

"Say 'I beg yer pardon,'" Maggie urged her sister.

"Ent beggin' her pardon for nuffink."

"That's quite all right, Miss Margaret," Claire assured her before fisticuffs ensued. "I am not offended. Let us be off. Master Jake, if you would be so kind as to accompany us, you may find it useful to memorize the list of ingredients as they are measured out. Since I do not have the use of my notebook."

He nodded, his face expressionless as this hint flew straight past his ears.

Ah well. She could hardly expect to reclaim all her things so soon.

They found a likely chemist in a lane just off Haymarket, in a neighborhood where Claire was unlikely to

see anyone she knew, but which received enough cus-
tom from people of quality that her accent would ensure there were no uncomfortable questions. At the
door, Claire turned to see a familiar form whisk itself
into the shadows further down the street. She schooled
her lips into serious lines. "Miss Maggie, would you be
so good as to invite your sister to join us? It is too bad
of an acquaintance of mine to behave like a footpad."

"She ent much of a footpad if *you* could see 'er,"
Jake pointed out.

Maggie ran off while she pushed open the door to
the shop, setting the bell over the door to ringing. Behind an oak counter blackened with age, the chemist
looked up from measuring a paper of powder. At the
sight of Jake, he frowned. "See here. Get away from
that lady, you. I'll have none of your thievery in here."

The place smelled of lemon, bitter herbs, and kero-
sene, and Claire fought the urge to sneeze. "This young
man is not a thief," she assured him in her plummiest
tones. "Nor is this boy, or these girls," she added as the
bell rang again and the Mopsies fell into the shop. "He
is here to assist me as part of his education."

The chemist did not dare contradict her, but his
gaze did not leave Jake's grubby hands as he said, "My
apologies, my lady. Many ladies of quality take an interest in the indigent. How may I help you this morning?"

Beside her, Jake bristled. He may not know what
indigent meant, but he certainly recognized the tone.
She laid a hand on his jacket sleeve. "We are pursuing
studies in the field of science, and my experiments re-

quire a number of chemicals." Beginning with the liquid capsaicin, she dictated a list of what she required, estimating the amounts of each from recent experience. She spoke slowly, so that the chemist could write them down, and Jake could commit them to memory.

"It will take me some time to measure these out, my lady. Boy!" he shouted.

Beside her, Willie jumped, though he had been doing nothing worse than pressing his nose against the glass of the case.

"Sir?" A young man even thinner than Snouts popped out of a door in the rear like a jack-in-the-box.

"Would you care for some tea while you wait, my lady?" the chemist inquired. "Robin will fetch it for you."

"How very kind. We should all love some, thank you."

The chemist looked flummoxed. "Er, so that would be—"

"Five cups. Thank you so much."

Ten minutes later found them seated with mugs of hot tea, sweet with honey and smoky with toasted jasmine. Lizzie and Willie slurped theirs with abandon, and Claire realized that lessons in deportment would need to be added to mathematics and science if they were to come out with her again. Maggie watched her every move, mimicking the way she held the mug, sipping when she sipped. When Willie drained his mug, Claire picked up the teapot. "May I offer you more?"

He shoved the mug closer, and Claire said to Maggie, "One goes to finishing school for months to learn how to pour tea gracefully, but the essence of the matter is this—your back must be straight, your shoulders lowered, and the speed of the pour is in direct proportion to the depth of the cup. In addition, you must never allow the spout to leak. If it does, the angle at which you are holding it is too steep." She filled Willie's cup without spilling a drop from the Brown Betty pot. "Would you like to try?"

Maggie swallowed the last of her tea and put it down, regarding the pot as one would a poisonous viper. "Pick it up by the handle, and rest your fingers upon the lid. In this way it will not fall off and land in your guest's cup. I can tell you from experience the consequences can be disastrous."

Fortunately, the pot was nearly empty and not very heavy. Maggie picked it up, held the lid on as if she were preventing a geyser from spouting out the top, and dribbled a quarter of it on the table before she got some into the mug that Jake pushed toward her.

"Thanks, Mags." As if having his tea poured by a lady were nothing out of the ordinary, Jake picked it up and took a long swallow.

"Well done, Maggie." Claire smiled as the girl put the pot down and sat back, blowing a long breath up through the nut-brown curls that fell in her face.

"She made a mess," Lizzie said angrily. "It weren't well done at all."

"Would you like to try?" Claire hadn't meant to be challenging, but Lizzie evidently took it that way. She snorted and grabbed the handle of the pot. But she underestimated its weight—the spout dipped—the lid fell off and smashed upon the tiles—and the entire pot slid from her hands and crashed upon the floor in an explosion of pottery shards and sodden tea leaves. Lizzie shrieked and burst into tears.

"Here, here, what's this?" The chemist and Robin erupted from the back of the shop, staring at the mess in dismay. "You ruffians, look what you've done!"

Claire rose, lengthening her neck and looking down upon him. "To whom are you referring?"

He blinked and flushed. "I didn't mean you, my lady. I meant—"

"Surely not my charges. I was attempting to give a lesson in deportment and we met with an accident. I will be happy to reimburse you for the cost of the pot and the tea. It was delicious and we enjoyed it very much."

It would also likely wipe out the few shillings she was hoping to save for something to eat, but there was nothing to be done about it. She could be grateful the tea had come their way unasked; her dehydrated body was reviving already.

Robin cleared away the mess while Maggie dragged her snuffling sister out into the street, where it was clear the latter was being read the Riot Act. Claire couldn't find it in her heart to stop her. Perhaps a remonstration from the sister she loved would do more to changing Lizzie's attitude than chapter and verse from anyone else.

The chemist tied up the vials and papers of chemicals into a neat parcel, and Claire handed over her precious two pounds. When a couple of shillings came back, it was all she could do not to snatch at them in case he changed his mind. Instead, she tucked them into her glove, gathered up her charges, and handed the parcel to Jake.

"Now," she said as they emerged from the lane onto Haymarket, "let's find lots of lovely things to eat while you, Master Jake, recite the contents of that parcel back to me."

As they went from the pie-seller to the sweet stall to the orange seller, Jake slowly and laboriously told over the list of chemicals, exactly as she had given it to the chemist. And when she finally—finally!—had a steak and kidney pie in her hands, she had to admit that his memory was faultless.

"Well done, Master Jake." She ate the pie out of her own palms, and nothing had ever tasted so good. "Well done indeed. Are you able to read and write, so that you can make the record permanent?"

"I know my letters."

"Good. Then I encourage you to possess yourself of a pencil at one of these stalls—paid for, if you please," she added hastily, as he made to reach for one on the sly. "I have paper in my satchel. You can begin your own compendium of chemical devices this very day."

He slid a glance at her as he handed over a half-penny for the pencil and put it in his pocket. "Don't seem very smart to be tellin' folk yer secrets."

"That was our agreement."

"Still. Folk'd pay big to know how to make them devices."

"Perhaps. Do you plan to sell that list to Billy Crumwell?"

He stopped, his eyes wide, and his free hand slid under the hem of his ragged jacket, where he kept his knife on his belt. "I ent no turncoat," he said in a low, dangerous tone.

Claire hoped he could not see her pulse pounding in her throat, and busied herself dusting crumbs off her hands and face. "I did not say you were. It seemed an odd thing for you to say, that's all."

"Tweren't me I meant. You could sell that list easy."

"I have no desire to sell it." She kept her voice admirably calm. "I would rather use it to better our circumstances. No, Willie, I'm afraid that if you have another sweet you will be sick. Perhaps you might look for something Rosie would enjoy."

"What's the matter wiv our circumstances?" Jake demanded.

"You must admit that rag-picking has its limits as a career," she told him. "If you were to focus your talents on chemistry, you might go farther."

"How'm I to do that?"

"I might be of assistance."

"Yer gonna disappear as sudden as you came. I don't know what yer playin' at, lady, but you don't belong wiv us."

Playing was the last word she would use to describe her situation. She swallowed the sharp retort on the tip of her tongue and said instead, "At the moment, our circumstances are remarkably similar. Rioters burned my house two days ago, Master Jake. It was in fleeing them that I came to your attention at the Aldgate station."

"What'd they do that for?"

"They thought my father owed them money. Except that he is dead and unable to pay." Jake snorted and Claire felt her cheeks cool with affront. "I find nothing amusing in that, sir."

"Oh, I do, lady. That's ezackly how I came to be on the streets."

"Where is your mother, then?"

"Dead."

"And you have no one?"

"Just Snouts and Tigg and the others."

"But no family?"

"Nope. You?"

"My mother is in Cornwall. She may as well be at the ends of the earth."

"I'm goin' t'the ends of the earth someday."

Unbidden, a smile tugged at her lips. "That's an admirable ambition, Master Jake. Shall you explore the Amazon, do you think?"

"Dunno. I'll most likely be transported for thieving."

With a sigh, Claire turned her attention to the whereabouts of her young charges. One thing at a time. He had not, after all, pulled the knife on her.

Yet.

22

The moon was no more than a possibility above the rooftops and catwalks of the docks when Claire finished compounding the gaseous capsaicin devices. By the light of a single stubby candle, Jake had recorded the ingredients and the steps by which they went together in laborious capitals, which meant that Claire worked much more slowly than usual. If she had had her notebook to hand, she could have completed the task in a quarter of an hour, but she stood more to gain by encouraging Jake's cooperation—not to mention the fact that here was an excellent opportunity for him to practice his letters and spelling.

Snouts ranged from doorway to doorway, his eye on the cobbled street on one side, and the river on the other. "Come on," he urged every five minutes. "They'll be long away before we get there."

Claire was at least as impatient as he; she was only better at concealing it. "We are ready, Mr. McTavish." She wrapped the vials carefully in what might once have been a tea towel before stowing them in her satchel. "Let's be off."

Billy Crumwell and his gang, it turned out, were the lords of a squat in St. Giles Close, an address that sounded much more aristocratic than it was thanks to its proximity to the impoverished St. Giles Church. All the same, it possessed a stone foundation, sturdy walls, and even an empty space in the back that had once aspired to being a garden.

"Does Billy Crumwell own this property?" Claire whispered to Snouts, crouching next to him in the shadows of the church's graveyard.

Snouts gave a snort, quickly muffled. "Don't nobody own it but who c'n 'ang onto it. Billy knifed Spotted Dick Black to get it, after 'e'd been in 'is gang for a year."

"But someone must own it."

"Ain't never seen 'em then. Them walls is gonna be trouble."

"What makes you say so?"

"'Ow you gonna loft them vials inside? I can only see one window what's broke. Mopsies!" The girls materialized next to them out of the dark. "Do a fast reconnoiter. We need 'oles in the walls, broken windows, and such like to pitch the vials through."

Without a sound, the girls vanished as though they had done this kind of thing before. Claire had done no more than spare a thought for how chilly the night was becoming when they reappeared. "There's a broken window next to the back door," Lizzie reported in a whisper. "Shingles ripped out of the roof on the river side, and a loose board on the other side. Front's tight and they set a watch."

Snouts swore at this intelligence. "Jake. You do the watch. Not a sound."

Claire clutched at Jake's arm. "What does that mean? You won't kill that person, will you?"

He gave her an incredulous look. "What d'you take me for? Not unless he gives me a fight."

"Not under any circumstances! I won't have my friends connected with murder."

"Lady—"

Claire's skin had gone cold with more than just the dewfall. "I will not have it, do you hear? We are to succeed through the exercise of intellect, not brute force."

"We'll succeed through t'exercise of my good right arm, Lady," Jake told her with flat scorn before he vanished into the night.

"I shall have words with him if any harm comes to the watch," she said with grim promise.

"Jake's a dab hand," Tigg assured her. "Watch won't feel a thing."

This did not have the comforting effect he obviously intended. However, there was nothing to be done except the job she had come to do. She gritted her teeth as Snouts directed their strategy. "Tigg, you're our best at the scramble, so you take the roof. I'll take the back door. Mopsies, you take Jake his vial and set our own watch. Lady, you'd best stay here."

"I shan't," Claire objected with no little warmth.

"You've done yer bit with the chemicals. You'll only be in the way."

"In the—? And who, might I ask, brought down your entire house at this very time last night with no assistance whatsoever?"

"Billy Crumwell's killed four men," Snouts's tone was as blunt as a bludgeon and just as effective. "We make one mistake and he'll do for us wi'out a thought. First sign of trouble, you take to your heels."

"I am not leaving without my landau—or any of you."

"Better you leave wi' yer life."

"But I—"

A bird whistled near the graveyard wall, and Snouts held up a hand. "Trouble." Inch by cautious inch, they peered around the flying angel monument behind which they were concealed, to see a lantern bob across the squat's yard. Three or four young men only a little older than Claire herself accompanied a person dressed in what appeared to be a velvet frock coat and a slightly crushed top hat adorned with a pair of driving goggles. His waistcoat was leather, and at his side he carried a rifle with a curiously bulbous and long barrel. Snouts drew a long breath.

"What? Who is that?" Claire whispered. "Is that Billy Crumwell?"

"Nah. Billy's the git in the long coat wi' the chains over 'is shoulder." Claire peered at the group more closely. She hadn't even noticed him. "That flash cove ... Lady, this is trouble. I'm callin' Jake and Maggie in."

"Why?"

Before he could answer, Billy Crumwell spoke to his companion. "I tell ye, Luke, ye won't be sorry. She's a beauty, not a scratch on 'er. A bargain at a hunnert pounds. Ye can go drivin' about and no one'll know you ent a lord."

Claire gripped the granite plinth. They were too late. That filthy criminal! "We have to follow them. They're about to sell my landau to that Luke person."

Snouts gave a very credible imitation of a sparrow, and within seconds Maggie had joined them. Not a moment too soon, either, because Luke and his four escorts hopped the wall where she had been posted and made their way through the graveyard not twenty feet away. They filed into the narrow alley between the church and the dilapidated tavern next to it. Claire rose and settled the satchel with its lethal contents on her back.

Snouts jerked her back down. "Lady, you can't. That's Lightning Luke Jackson."

"For heaven's sake, let go of my skirt. I don't care if it's the leader of the Opposition. We'll lose them!"

Jake dove into the shadow of the monument, breathing hard. "Good call, Snouts. Watch is out, but you won't catch me takin' on Lightning Luke."

She neither knew nor cared what or who Lightning Luke Jackson was. All she knew was that he was about to buy her landau out from under her, and she had not come this far nor lost this much to allow it. "We are armed. I'm following them. You may do as you like."

Ducking low and moving from monument to headstone, Claire clutched her hat, dodged across the graveyard and plunged into the inky shadow of the alley, where the voices ahead told her that her quarry had no fear of pursuit.

She smiled, guiding herself with fingertips on the greasy, cold wall to her right. A sound behind her wiped the smile away and she whirled to find a small form silhouetted against the moonlight. "Maggie?" A second form joined the first. "Lizzie?" Both girls pressed themselves against her skirts, even as she forged ahead with as much stealth as she could muster. "What are you doing? Has Snouts relented?"

"E's in a fury," Maggie whispered with admirable economy. "But I couldn't let you go by yerself. We're flock mates."

"An' I'm her flock mate." Lizzie evidently wanted no confusion as to where her loyalties lay. "Mind you don't get 'er kilt."

"I will do my utmost to prevent that," Claire promised. "Now. No more talking. We have work to do."

23

Two streets closer to the river, a row of warehouses stood hunched over a thoroughfare so narrow it might as well have been an alley. Down the middle of the cobbles ran a thin stream of filthy water, carrying with it bits of flotsam and food so rotted even the scurrying rats wouldn't stop for it. Deplorable though her skirts might be, Claire lifted them and hugged the side of the building as the three of them kept their quarry in sight. They crouched behind a pile of barrels where the alley opened out into a square.

"No cover," Lizzie whispered. "Best to wait 'ere."

Billy Crumwell led the way to a low, arched door, with just enough clearance for a wagon. "In here. Won't no one disturb us this time of night."

In her stealthy pursuit, Claire had hatched a plan. The Mopsies huddled together next to her, and she leaned close. "As soon as they're all inside, I shall use the gaseous capsaicin. Cover your faces with your skirts. Do not breathe it."

"Let us have a look first."

"No, I—"

Too late. With no more sound than a rustle of limp rags, the girls darted between the buildings, in a space barely wide enough for a skinny dog to pass. To her horror, she heard the landau's top make the familiar shivery sound as it folded back, and in the next moment, someone dropped the hood and swore.

They were trying to ignite it. Heaven knew what havoc their untrained hands would wreak, messing about with boiler and coal. They would unbalance the entire mechanism, and then she would be unable to pilot it out of this noisome place.

As fast as her fingers would move, she retrieved two of the devices from their wrappings in the satchel, slung it back on, and slipped over to the door. Not one guard stood outside. Fools. By leaning mere inches to the left, she could see around the door. There was her landau, a sheet of canvas crumpled on the floor next to it. Someone had got the hood up again, and two of the thieves had their heads inside, trying to figure out how to ignite it, while a third sat in the driver's seat, her own goggles perched on his head.

She tightened her lips, and when someone touched her hand, she jumped half a foot and let out a squeak.

"Warehouse fronts on t'river," Maggie whispered rapidly. "If we gots to run, tide's out."

Before Claire could puzzle out the connection between these two facts, someone shouted from inside. "Hey! Who's that? Jim, get the door."

"We're spotted!" Maggie grabbed her hand. "This way."

"No." As hard as she could, Claire flung first one, then the other device to either side of the landau. As they shattered on the floor, she grabbed the door. "Maggie, help me!"

They pushed it shut just as a body hit the other side, and Claire hung onto the slats for dear life. She pulled at the iron bar that had once rested across the front, but to no avail. The door began to open, inexorably pushing her out into the square. Another body hit the back of it, and another, and the door was flung back. She stumbled to the side as Lightning Luke careened into the open, his hands mashed to his eyes, his oddly shaped gun in the crook of his elbow and hanging over his forearm. Shrieking in pain, the others followed, a cloud of gas billowing out behind them.

Luke collapsed not ten feet from her, the flared barrel of the gun clunking on the cobbles next to him.

The gun. That was what everyone feared most.

She darted forward and snatched it up, then nearly fell headlong herself as its unexpected weight dragged at her arms. Luke did not move except to moan and scrub at his eyes with the velvet tails of his coat. She hefted his gun more carefully, and in the swath of lamplight that fell out into the middle of the square, eyed its operation.

It possessed a trigger, but there was no chamber for bullets. Not like her father's pistols. But what was this? Instead of a chamber, there was a thick glass globe. If she moved this lever, then ...

The gun began to hum.

Now what was she to do? Common sense begged her to ignite the landau and drive away as fast as she could. But where was Lizzie? Maggie had taken refuge again behind the barrels. She could not leave without the other child, but if she didn't begin the landau's ignition sequence immediately, the miscreants would recover and her situation would be unthinkable.

A dim reflection of blue light pulsed on the wet cobbles. She looked down.

A lightning storm had formed in the glass globe, and the hum had taken on real authority now. Great heavens, this gun somehow harnessed electrick power! No wonder they called him Lightning Luke.

She had to move. Now.

"Maggie," she shouted. "Find Lizzie!"

"Who's that?" Luke had gotten to his feet, and swayed like a drunken man. "Where's my gun?"

He was still blinded. Common sense told her to keep quiet, get the landau started, and get out of there. Anger demanded that she give him a piece of her mind.

"It's a trap," one of his companions moaned. "Billy's done turned on us."

Luke got one eye open, which widened at the sight of her, then slammed shut as droplets of condensed capsaicin gas rolled into it. "Who are you? Put that down, you fool of a woman, and get out of here."

With the help of the side of the building nearest her, Billy had managed to stand as well. One of Luke's men flung himself at him. "Turncoat! You'll see us all dead!"

He pulled a knife, and before Claire could even shriek, he had stabbed Billy in the chest. The chains laced through the shoulders of his long coat clanked on the cobbles as he fell. Instinctively, her hands tightened on the gun, her forefinger sliding into the trigger guard, and when Billy rolled, his still twitching arm slapped her skirts. She screamed, lurched back, and the gun went off.

A lightning bolt ten feet long leaped from the flared barrel, flashing across the square and catching Luke dead in the center of his chest. He arched back as flickering tendrils of blue light traveled outward, along his limbs, along his coat, even to the top of his crushed beaver hat. His eyes bugged out and there was a sizzling sound as the liquid in them evaporated. He fell, rigid as a tree trunk, and lay still.

A plume of smoke rose from the blackened mass that had been his leather vest.

Claire's fingers went numb, and she dropped the gun on her foot. The night crowded into her vision, and a hive of bees seemed to have entered her brain. From a great distance, she heard another shout that sounded like, "Lady! Are you all right?" and several figures ran into the square.

Fisticuffs.

The Mopsies.

If there was fighting, they would be in danger. She must not faint. She must not.

The gun will hurt them. Pick up the gun. Get the landau. Find the Mopsies.

"Lady!"

She blinked and Snouts's face swam into clarity. "Mr. McTavish?"

"Stop standing there like a mug, Lady. You just kilt Lightning Luke Jackson!"

"Is he ... really dead?" Surely not. This had not happened. She would wake in her comfortable bed in Wilton Crescent presently and wonder what she had eaten to cause such vivid dreams.

"As a blinkin' doornail." Dream or not, Snouts was speaking slowly and not allowing her gaze to wander from his. "Look sharp, Lady. We have to get back to his squat before word gets out and the bobbies come."

"Squat? What for?"

"He's got a house, Lady. A real house, wiv a door and chimbley and everything. And rugs, so I hear. We've got to get there and claim it afore the rats come out' the woodwork and take it."

"What has his house to do with us?" Her mind felt like cotton wool. She could not connect sentences into meaning.

Snouts took her arm—the one not cradling the gun—and walked her back into the warehouse where the landau sat. "Here's how it works. You kilt him—"

"I didn't mean to, Snouts. The gun went off by accident."

"Beggin' yer pardon, Lady, but you just keep mum about that. Story is, you disarmed Lightning Luke and shot him for stealin' your property. Maybe you knifed Billy Crumwell, too, for all I know."

"Luke's man did it. It was shocking."

"That's neither here nor there, and neither are they. Point is, he who takes down Lightning Luke gets his property, see? Jake!" he called into the dark. "Round everyone up. We've got a body to get over to Vauxhall Gardens for proof, soon's we get this landau going."

Ah, here was something solid to count on. Something she knew how to do. With the smoothness of long habit, she pulled her duster from its niche and buttoned it over her suit. By the light of the lamp the thieves had lit to admire her property, she saw her goggles lying on the floor where they had evidently been flung when the thief had run for it. She settled them over her eyes and began the ignition sequence. When the indicator needles jumped, she lit the headlamps. Snouts dumped Lightning Luke's rigid body on the canvas and rolled him up in it, then tied the bundle to the rear guard with a length of rope.

"What about—him?" She indicated Billy Crumwell's inert form out in the square. "We can't just leave him there."

"Pickers'll do fer 'im before dawn," Snouts said with chilling brevity while he divested the man of his perfectly usable leather coat. He and Maggie squeezed into Gorse's usual seat, and Jake, Tigg, and Lizzie piled into the rear compartment, which was meant only for parcels.

LADY OF DEVICES

As smoothly as though she were driving to Regent's Park, she applied steam and they rolled out the warehouse door, leaving behind the deserted square—empty except for the silence of the grave and the smell of bridges well and truly burned.

Vauxhall Gardens was not nearly as picturesque as its name might suggest. Claire guided the landau down one narrow street after another at Snouts's direction, winding deeper into the neighborhoods of the working poor. At least they had proper roofs over their heads, unlike the children packed all around her, who had to make do with a warehouse loft.

"There." Snouts pointed to a stone house nestled against the bridge abutment. Possessed of two storeys, its windows were intact and even at this hour, light glowed behind the ones downstairs. "It fronts on the river, so Luke can move his cargo."

"What cargo?"

"Dunno. Whatever he lifted that day, I suppose. He started out a rag picker like us, they say, but bein' the enterprisin' sort, he moved up in the world. I figure piracy and theft, but them's the sorts of questions a man don't ask down here."

"I hope his associates don't expect those activities to continue." Claire appraised the house as the landau coasted to a stop in front. It was a solid little place. Nothing was broken or abused—in fact, if a criminal could be said to be house-proud, then Lightning Luke was that. Even the head-high stone wall around what could have been a front garden was sturdy and well kept.

Just how sturdy, they discovered as soon as they approached. "There's no gate," Maggie said. "'Ow are we to get in?"

"On the river side," Jake said. "Best scout it first."

The Mopsies took their duties very seriously, and even if Claire had wanted to protest, her voice would have had less effect than the gurgle of the river against the stone arches of the bridge. On the house's other side was a tangle of brambles and what might have been a toll shed for the drawbridge, now fallen into disrepair. So Luke's house might once have belonged to the toll keeper.

The Mopsies returned with silent suddenness. "Watch is posted," Lizzie said. "There's a platform above the people door an' a bloke wi' a bl—er, a dirty big gun. Water door's shut and locked tight. Windows too."

"We can't use the gassy—gassicky—" Maggie stopped.

"Gaseous capsaicin devices," Claire finished. "It does not seem so. Our plan, then?"

Jake snorted in a most ungentlemanly fashion. "Lady, you're the mort wi' the gun. Ent no one gonna argue wi' you. Take out the watch wi' one shot and after that the place is ours."

Claire felt her jaw slacken with horror, and firmed both it and her resolution. "We shall not. There will be no murder."

"What d'ye call Lightning Luke's situation, then?" Tigg wanted to know.

"As I've already explained, that was an accident. And since Mr. Jake is a 'dab hand' at such things, I suggest he take care of the watch."

Jake put a hand on Lizzie's shoulder. "What sort o' gun was it?"

"One o' them many-chambered ones that go round and round."

Snouts made a sound of disbelief. "Them ones wot were invented by that nasty Gatling bloke? If that's true, no one's getting in that way. We'll have to do for the river door."

"And what's to prevent him shooting us no matter what door we use?" Claire had not wanted to come on this fool's errand, but she was not about to be held up at the gates if the inside of Luke's house was as snug as the outside. What if there was food? And a basin to wash in?

And to what depths had she sunk when the merest possibility of such amenities would make her contemplate violence?

"Enough. We shall announce our presence like civilized people, show them Luke's body, and the house will be ours. Isn't that what you said, Mr. McTavish?"

Snouts hesitated. "It might be a tad more dodgy than that, Lady."

"Why?"

"What's to stop 'em from just shooting us fer killin' their boss?"

It took Claire a full ten seconds to reel in her temper and exhaustion and to curtail the urge to slap him. "Why did you not bring up this possibility before?"

"'Cause maybe you wouldn't have come?"

Claire turned her back on him and marched along the wall in the direction of the river. Behind her, a muffled conversation broke out, and then silence. When she risked a glance back, she could see nothing but two small shadows and a larger one against the deeper dark of the stone wall. Why the presence of two ten-year-old ragamuffins and a boy of twelve should make her confidence rise was more than she could explain. Still, if a person was going to march up to an armed establishment with a pathetic plan, it was comforting to know she was not alone. And just to be prudent, she flipped the lever on the lightning rifle. Its hum and the accompanying vibration in her hands was comfort of a different sort.

It felt good to be in command of something. Electrick power was nothing to sneeze at. She had no intention of hurting anyone, but she would not be treated like a nonentity again.

She peered around the corner of the wall and found the Mopsies' reconnaissance report to be accurate. On a verandah above the door, a deadly looking example of one of Mr. Gatling's guns stood mounted on a swivel. Behind it lounged an individual who clearly did not expect to be challenged.

"Ho! You there!" she called.

In the light from the window behind him, she saw him jump and swing his feet down from the railing. Leaping to battle position, he commanded, "State yer errand."

"My errand is to require your unconditional surrender." The lightning rifle had begun to sound like it meant business.

"Sez who?"

"Sez the Lady of Devices, 'oo shot down Lightning Luke wiv 'is own gun," came Jake's voice from behind her. "Show yer hands and come down."

In answer, the guard grasped something in the back of his weapon, and the multiple bores swung to face them. "I'll show ye more'n my hands, you pitiful lot."

Claire's instincts for self-preservation had not been honed by her previous life, but in that moment she discovered they were alive and well in her current one. She swung the lightning rifle to bear on the sullen barrels of the gun above her, and pulled the trigger.

The bolt sizzled wide and fried the railing two feet to the guard's left. While he shouted, she corrected its trajectory and fired again. This time the bolt swallowed the Gatling piece in its lethal blue light, the tiny wriggling currents of power seizing it and stopping its action. The cartridges in the magazine began to explode like Cantonese fireworks. Claire and Jake grabbed the Mopsies and flung themselves under the verandah as, screaming and maddened with pain, the guard leaped into the sullen waters of the Thames below.

"Now, lady!" Tigg and Snouts rushed past her—oh, he condescended to join them, did he, now that the field was hers?—and burst through the front door. The commotion outside had alerted everyone within that something was amiss, and a bullet pinged off the door frame inches from her head.

"Stand aside!" she shouted, and when her crew pressed themselves against the wall, she sent a lightning bolt into the large room on the right, aiming at the fireplace. In the blue flash, the lamplight erased itself and time stopped, as though a flicker at the theater had frozen on a single image. Horrified faces. Bodies flung upon the floor. A rug. A sofa.

"I require your immediate and unconditional surrender," she announced amid the smell of burned stone and the shrieks and whimpers of the unprepared. "I am the Lady of Devices, and I claim this house as my own. Lightning Luke is dead and I have his body outside. If you are unable to accept my terms, I will allow you to leave. But if you stay, I demand your loyalty. Make your choice now."

No one moved.

In the silence, a muffled voice asked, "You kilt Lightning Luke? For true?"

"It's true." Snouts stepped forward, looking as though he were inspecting a battalion. "I saw it meself. The Lady's a fair leader, and I'm her first lieutenant."

"You're not first anything, Snouts McTavish." A boy who couldn't be any older than Jake pushed himself up off the floor. "You're a thief and a rag picker and I ent belonging to any gang wot has you in it."

"That is perfectly fair." With the flared barrel of the rifle, Claire gestured toward the door. "You may leave unaccosted."

Snouts bristled at her failure to defend his honor, but for once, in the interests of solidarity, kept his mouth shut. The boy looked about him at his prostrate companions. "Are you lot gonna just lie there and let 'em take over? Anybody gets Luke's treasury, it's us wot worked for it, not them."

Treasury?

Slights to his manhood forgotten, she and Snouts exchanged a glance. Without a word, the Mopsies disappeared. Scouts to their fingertips, they did not need to be told where their duty lay.

"The treasury belongs to those who have earned it," she said loudly. "And believe me, if you stay under my—" Command? Jurisdiction? "—roof, you will earn it. There will be no more thieving and fisticuffs and pickpocketing. We will earn our bread through the force of intellect, as befits ladies and gentlemen of this modern age."

Murmuring rose from the corners of the room, and people began to get up, keeping one eye on the lightning rifle as they did so. A handful of them—goodness, the eldest couldn't be more than her own age—sidled past her and out the door.

"A pity a life on the correct side of the law does not appeal," she observed to no one in particular.

"Ent much money in it to most folk," Jake responded. Then his voice grew stronger, pitched to the back of the room. "Shame they ent schooled in the ways of your devices, not to mention your foolproof stratagems at cards, innit? All the more for us, I say."

The slow trickle out of the room halted.

"Devices? Stratagems?" asked a boy with a mop of curly hair, mummified to the chin in an enormous woolen muffler. "Like them Wits?"

"The Lady is a Wit leader," Jake said without a twitch. "We already took down Billy Crumwell's gang afore we got around to Lightning Luke's. I'ze you, I'd stick to the winning side."

"It's for true, then," the boy whispered. "She really kilt 'im." His gaze traveled the length of Luke's rifle in Claire's hands. "Her own self."

"'Is corpse is outside, you don't believe 'er," Jake told him. "But touch the Lady's landau an' it's worth your life."

"I recommend we give your former leader a decent burial." Claire took command of the situation before the tales got any taller. "Is there any among you who would like to say a few words?" No one moved. Evidently he was not held in high regard among his confederates. How did one go about burying the man one had accidentally killed? "Are we possessed of a shovel?"

Snouts nudged her. "You leave that to me, Lady. Once I'm done, no one will ever know what happened to 'im. You'd best see to that treasury quick-like, in case any here gets ideas above their station, as it were."

"Quite right, Mr. McTavish." She turned on her heel and, accompanied by Jake and Tigg, went in search of the Mopsies. Perhaps on her way to the treasury she might happen upon some food.

LADY OF DEVICES

25

With Tigg in the passenger seat in charge of the lightning rifle, Claire piloted the landau back through sleeping London to fetch Weeping Willie and Rosie the
chicken from the warehouse, where the former had been
guarding the latter with all seriousness. On the way
back, Tigg regaled the smaller boy with the story of
their exploits. Willie turned upon her a look of horror
mixed with admiration.

Claire's heart twisted with remorse. "I did not kill
Mr. Jackson on purpose, Willie," she said as gently as
she could, watching the street while she drove. Drat
Tigg and his stories unsuitable for tender ears. "I'm
afraid the lightning rifle fired by accident. And it won't
happen again, I promise you."

"Don't make promises you can't keep, Lady," Tigg warned. "It's a hard life, wot we got."

"No one knows that better than I," she said with utter sincerity. "Which is why I shall do everything in my power to improve it for all our sakes."

How that was to be accomplished was unclear at present, but she possessed a mind that relished such a challenge. At the moment, though, all she could think of was finding a quiet corner in which to sleep. She asked Snouts to set a watch on the landau to prevent its being stolen again. Then she, Willie, the Mopsies, and Rosie retired to the topmost room in the house, which featured bare wood floors, rather a lot of dust— and an actual lock upon the door.

"Tomorrow every single one of us shall clean this place from top to bottom," she vowed. "And then I am tempted to return to Wilton Crescent to steal my own bed."

The remnants of Lightning Luke's gang soon found out she was a woman of her word. And in the course of their cleaning—amid mutters of mutiny—they discovered the wage of a good morning's work. Claire had set the mother's helper in motion in the upstairs room, and when she climbed the ladderlike stair to fetch it down to the next floor, she found the Mopsies bent over it, murmuring.

"What is it, ladies?"

Maggie straightened. "This device of yours, Lady. I think it's 'ad a knock on its noggin."

Claire bent to examine it. Repeatedly, it bumped against the wall, in the manner of a goldfish who does not realize it cannot pass through solid matter to escape its prison. How odd. "It is supposed to turn aside when it meets resistance," she said to the girls. "I have never seen it do this before."

"'Ow does it know it's to turn aside?" Lizzie asked.

"With statick repulsion—rather like what happens when you put the wrong ends of magnets together." At Lizzie's blank face, Claire realized she would need to add rudimentary physics to the young lady's education. "A solid object will intrude upon the statick field and cause the device to turn aside."

"P'raps that wall ent solid." Lizzie and Maggie stared at one another, wide-eyed. Then as one, they attacked. Claire had no more than raised a hand to stop them when a panel tilted backward, hinged from the top, and the girls tumbled headlong into the opening.

"Lady! Give us a light," came a muffled voice. When Claire had fetched a lamp and Snouts, in case male assistance should be needed, they found the girls sitting on either side of an ironbound chest. "That's why he had a lock on t'door," Maggie told her with shining eyes. "'Ow we goin' to open this mucky great strongbox?"

Together they dragged it back through the opening into the larger room. "Lucky job I checked Lightning Luke's waistcoat afore I laid 'im t'rest." Snouts pulled a small iron key from his pocket, popped the lock open, and lifted the lid. Maggie reached in and sifted pennies, crowns, and shillings through her fingers, her face slack with wonder.

"Well done, ladies." Claire did not want to think about Luke's final resting-place. She did not want to think about Luke or his demise at all. Not after the horrible dreams that had wakened her in the wee hours and stolen what sleep was left of the night. "You deserve every half-penny. Keep as much as you can carry in both hands."

"'Twere the mother's helper did it." Lizzie regarded the device, now busy with the filthy plank floor of the room, with newfound respect. "P'raps it will find summat more'n dirt on t'other floor, too. Best we stick by it."

Claire divided half of Luke's ill-gotten gains among everyone in the house—which proved to be an excellent lesson in arithmetic for Jake and Tigg, who led the effort. "I shall take the other half to the bank," she told Snouts privately, "and invest it in the railroads and the Royal Society of Engineers until we decide what to do with it. Personally, I think we should give it to the Society for the Protection of War Widows and Orphans. I am quite sure Mr. Jackson was responsible for the poverty of at least some of them."

He gave her a doubtful look. "You'll 'ave an 'ard time convincin' this lot the widows an' orphans deserve it more than they do. They'll just think you stole it."

She raised her chin. "I shan't tolerate having my motives questioned. They have seen how fairly I deal. They will just have to trust me. Besides, none of this is really ours, Snouts. We *have* stolen it, not to put too fine a point on things."

"Spoils of war, Lady," he told her roughly. "Don't look a gift horse in the mouth. At least this roof don't leak, an' there's enough artillery in the cellar to hold off anyone who disagrees wiv' us for a month should it come to that."

"It will not. We will not give the criminals and the thieves of London any competition. We shall set our sights on a different arena entirely."

With the comforting weight of money in her skirt pocket, she hired a carter with a steam-powered dray and returned to Wilton Crescent. It stood just as she'd left it, except that the note was missing from the sink, as was everything but the bedstead in Mrs. Morven's room. Ah. That worthy lady must have relocated to Lord James's establishment. At least she would be safe there. Claire directed the carter and his burly boy to load up every single other thing left in the house, including the bedstead, the linens, and the piano.

What of Gorse, then? He must have gone to the Wellesleys. Claire added *Send tubes to Gorse and Mrs. Morven* to the mental list that included *See Mr. Arundel about who owns the cottage* and *Eat something.* The cottage in Vauxhall Gardens might not be much, but it possessed a vacuum tube. With that, she could communicate and keep a tenuous thread connecting herself with her old world.

Claire had been trained practically since infancy in how to run a household. Or to be more accurate, her mother had led by example and Claire had taken refuge in books and experiments. She regretted now that she had not paid more attention to the practice of housewifery. Of course, the art of drawing up the menu for a dinner party of eighteen was slightly different from arranging the trip to market that would result in the production of food on the table for the same number. She doubted that Lady St. Ives had ever been to market in her life, much less in the company of a gang of cutpurses and street children who saw no harm in lifting an orange if they could get away with it. In their view, the sin lay in being caught.

But at the very least, writing out the list of items to be purchased each day gave the Mopsies practice in their letters, and each of them possessed such a sharp mind that they were never shorted by so much as a penny during the actual purchase.

The boy who had been so scornful of Snouts on the night they'd claimed the house—who introduced himself to Claire as Lewis but was called Loser by everyone else—proved to be a helpful ally once he realized that the Lady meant business and tolerated no nonsense. The disloyal were invited to leave, and as her reputation spread, the number of volunteers knocking at the river door became rather gratifying. Lewis flushed an ancient crone out of the warren of streets whom he claimed to be his grandmother. She may have moved at the pace of a stick insect, but she could cook, and as long as the larder was kept stocked, meals appeared at more or less regular intervals. They had no table to put them on at first, but one evening four of the boys came puffing along the bridge above the house bearing a ten-foot dining table that they claimed had fallen out of a boat. Claire closed her eyes and beckoned them in, and the table became headquarters for the poker players when it was off duty.

A full stomach and productive activity went a long way to ensuring the loyalty of the remaining doubters in her abilities.

It went a long way to easing the knot of tension between Claire's shoulders, too. She was managing. With no tools but her mind and no prospects but those she was able to open up herself, she was actually managing to create order out of chaos. The fact that accidental murder had opened up these gates of possibility was not lost on her. Not an hour passed that she did not look out at the river or the road, convinced that a party of vengeful criminals—or a steambus of Mr. Peel's bobbies—were on their way to demand justice. But at this moment, as she piloted the landau back to Vauxhall Gardens behind the chugging dray with one eye on the road and the other on the balance of the piano, she reflected that circumstances could certainly be much, much worse.

She could be in gaol. She could be lying dead in the street.

She could be doing needlework in the dim, sunless parlor belonging to her grand-aunts Beaton.

26

Over the next week, her motley household settled into its own peculiar rhythm. Mornings were dedicated to market, with accompanying lessons in economics and mathematics. Afternoons were devoted to sharpening the skills of the card players and to the introduction of chemistry and physics. Here Jake's photographic memory proved invaluable—and it was he who, on the Wednesday after their arrival, finally returned her engineering notebook, her pencils, and dear Linnaeus to her.

"I figure you ent gonna cut out on us now, Lady," he said gruffly as he handed them over.

"No." She clutched the books to her chest, resisting the urge to check that no pages had gone missing. "I'm glad to see your confidence in my character is improving."

He shook his head, and his chocolate-brown eyes met hers. "You either keeps yer word or I goes to the bobbies and tell 'em it was you what kilt Lightning Luke."

Clearly she did not have to look as far as the road or the river for justice to be meted out to her. She was harboring it right here.

Since the kitchen was now the sole domain of Granny Protheroe, with occasional incursions permitted by Claire and the Mopsies should they be bearing groceries, the front parlor became the laboratory. No more did boys lounge on sofa and floor, drinking rotgut, smoking, and staying out of range of Luke's gun. Instead, glass tubes and flasks appeared, along with retorts, Bunsen burners, and cells for the creation of electrick current.

Claire had no idea who had built Lightning Luke's gun, but he or she had obviously been a genius. Her first task was to discover the source of its power. If she could replicate it, then they could make other devices and sell them. She would not be so silly as to replicate the rifle itself—she was neither metallurgist nor fool— but there were other mechanisms that might be devised.

In the meantime, her sketches and equations had to be translated into terms that her ragged compatriots could understand. Some gave up and joined Snouts at the card table. But some, like Jake, persevered even in the face of repeated failure, stubborn as stones and unwilling to allow capricious numbers and persnickety measurements to defeat them. Jake had the makings of a fine chemist. What a pity she had to fight his mistrust at every turn. Ah well. If she could not create a friend where none had been, then at the very least she would create a capable assistant.

In the evenings the poker players scattered to their chosen fields of labor. There they learned variations on the venerable cowboy poker, or invented them, and taught the others when they returned. One of Snouts's variations in particular, Old Blind Jack, suddenly became the rage in even the most fashionable of London's card rooms, to the point that strategy diagrams began to appear on the back page of the *Evening Standard* where illustrations of classic chess moves had held court for years.

Snouts just chuckled and bought his very first velvet waistcoat, tailored to fit.

Upon seeing it the Mopsies immediately demanded their own finery, and Snouts magnanimously handed over twenty pounds as though it were nothing. Claire had seen the account book they'd cobbled together out of the end papers of her books from Wilton Crescent, and in comparison to the money flowing through the boy's clever hands, twenty pounds *was* next to nothing.

On the next sunny Saturday, Claire took the Mopsies, Tigg, and Willie to Fortnum & Mason to have them outfitted. Never again would she allow the likes of the chemist in the Haymarket to look at her charges in that manner. And once the salesladies had removed the children's old clothes to the dustbin, their mouths pruned in disgust, and dressed them from the skin out in clean linen, cotton, and lace for the girls, and practical navy wool for the boys, Claire beamed at them proudly.

"You look as though you were visiting from Buckingham Palace itself." She smoothed Willie's sailor collar so that it lay flat across his shoulders. "Even Her Majesty's grandchildren don't look as fine as you."

"The Princess Alice chose that very dress for her youngest," the saleslady confided, nodding in Lizzie's direction. "She took the blue hair ribbons, though, instead of the coral."

Lizzie wavered visibly.

"Have the blue as well, if you like," Claire told her. "Snou—I mean, Mr. McTavish would approve."

Upon their return to the river cottage Claire discovered that Lizzie was in unrepentant possession of the saleslady's purse, having picked her pocket as the lady was dressing her.

The chill of disappointment warred with the heat of anger as Claire fought to keep her voice steady. "This is unacceptable." Her tone was deadly quiet—so quiet, in fact, that Lizzie made the mistake of believing Claire was not serious.

"'Twere easy," she said, swinging the pitifully small purse back and forth. "She leaned over to tie me sash and there it was, in front of me nose."

"You will return it immediately."

Lizzie gave her a look of disgusted disbelief. "Shan't."

Before the girl could do more than whip the purse back into her own pocket, Claire had snatched her off her feet and again applied the laws of physics in vigorous fashion. In the resulting uproar, the chemists reached protectively for their vials of liquids, and the card players froze with their cards pressed to their chests.

Unfortunately for Lizzie, her fine new underclothes were no match for the force of Claire's temper, and when the girl was reduced to a sniveling, just barely repentant huddle on the floor, Claire said in a tone not one note removed from the one she'd used previously, "We shall leave immediately for Fortnum's, where you shall return that purse."

Mumble.

"I beg your pardon, Miss Elizabeth?"

"What'm I to tell 'er?"

"The truth, of course."

"She'll call t'bobbies for sure and it'll be your fault if I land up in the clink."

"You could say you found it on t'ground," Maggie put in helpfully.

"And add lying to thievery?" Maggie quailed at the control in Claire's voice. Claire would never have believed that of all the things her mother had taught her, how to infuse deadly force into one's voice without raising it was the last she would have expected to find so useful.

"No, Lady." Maggie's lips trembled, both from shame and from fear for her sister's liberty.

"You are young ladies now," Claire said, allowing a touch of gentleness to creep in. "You make your way through the application of intelligence, grace, and consideration for others. You do the right thing, not the easy thing. I suggest you use the time it takes to drive back into town to compose an appropriately humble and truthful address to the purse's owner."

When they had located the young lady in question, it was clear she had just discovered the absence of her purse. "I beg your pardon, miss, but I'm all of a flutter. I—I seem to have—that is, I've lost—and I was just paid, too." Her enormous brown eyes filled with tears before she got herself under control. "Is there something else you wished me to help you with?"

"My young charge has something to tell you." With an inexorable hand between her shoulder blades, Claire pressed Lizzie forward.

The girl held up the little leather purse and the sales lady gasped as she took it. "Oh, thank you! What a precious child! You have given me such relief!" She swept Lizzie into her arms and hugged her so hard that Lizzie's cheeks turned bright pink.

"Miss, I—" she tried to speak, but the saleslady covered her face in kisses. With a final "Thank you!" she bustled through a door in the back, leaving Lizzie with her fine speech trembling on her tongue, unsaid. She turned a beseeching face to Claire. "I tried, Lady, but she wouldn't let me."

"You have received thanks you did not deserve, and forgiveness that you did." Claire touched the wide ribbon in her hair. "It took courage to make the attempt, and I salute you for it."

Lizzie and Maggie shared the front seat all the way home, holding hands and considerably lighter of heart than on the trip in. Claire was no judge of how to bring up children, but she was a fair judge of character. The tension of that ride to town would go a long way to preventing Lizzie from exercising her light fingers again. At the very least, she'd seen the effect thievery could have on someone who was barely more fortunate than herself. The loss of a week's wages would have hurt that young woman deeply, and Lizzie was headstrong, not heartless.

Dear me. Mathematics and chemistry are so much more straightforward. How have I managed to become a ramshackle sort of mother when I'm mere weeks out of school myself?

But there was no use wondering about the strangeness of her lot. She had killed a man, even if she hadn't meant to. If she could turn these ragamuffin children into useful young men and ladies, maybe it would go some way toward paying back that debt. She may as well play the mother. After all, with every day that passed here on the wrong side of the river, the likelihood that any man would want to wed her faded further away. She had no prospects and now possessed what could only politely be called a "past." If with God's aid she could help these children, maybe she would have done as much good as any real mother in London.

27

If she held onto her hat, Claire could tilt her head wa-a-ay back and take in the topmost panes of the immense Crystal Palace. Beside her, Lizzie did the same, lost her balance, and staggered backward into Tigg's arms.

"Steady on," he said, setting her on her feet. "Don't want to tumble into any of these engines."

"'Ow tall is it?" Claire had never seen the girl so awestruck. "Does it touch the clouds?"

"It might if it were raining." Claire consulted the guidebook. "It says here the top of that rounded roof is one hundred and eight feet. So if you took seven houses like ours and stacked them one on top of each other, you'd just be able to climb up and touch the glass."

"I ent climbin' up any such for all the tea in China."

"I'm very glad to hear it. Shall we go look at the steam engines?"

Making their way through the crowds of people, it took some time to get to the exhibit hall. Half the spectators were looking at the exhibits and the other half were gazing up and down the long vistas of glass, holding their hats as Claire had done. While Willie and Tigg examined a small engine to pull wagonloads of coal or tin, Claire stood next to an enormous steam locomotive and gazed at it with as much awe as Lizzie had the glassed-over sky.

How was it possible that such power and intricacy could be so beautiful? And how was she going to gain admission to the university so that she too could one day create something as huge and inspiring as this?

"I see our interests coincide once more," said a male voice beside her.

If he had left off the last two words, Claire would have cut the man dead for his impertinence and moved away to collect the children. As it was, she blinked up at him from under her impractical but very pretty hat brim.

Of all the people ... ! "Mr. Malvern."

"I must confess how happy I am to see you. Did you get my card?"

Concerned. "I did. What did you mean by it, sir?"

He hesitated, evidently expecting her to swoon like the schoolgirl his partner believed her to be. "Simply that I was worried about you. The papers were full of the Belgravia riots. When I could get no news of you, I went to the house. I left a message with the dustman."

Ah. Mystery solved.

Goodness. He traveled all the way from his laboratory to Belgravia simply to see if she was safe? How kind. And how very singular. "You have no need to worry. I am quite well."

"I see that."

Tigg drifted to her side and Claire resisted the urge to smile at his protectiveness.

Andrew Malvern tensed under his conservatively cut suit. "I say. Not so close to the lady, if you please."

Claire laid a hand on Tigg's arm before he did something foolish, like attempt fisticuffs. "It's quite all right. Mr. Tigg is with me, as are the three children examining that engine behind you."

"With you?" Mr. Malvern's gaze went from the Mopsies and Willie in their clothes fit for a queen's grandchildren, to Tigg, who had not consented to dress for the occasion, in his ragged pants and jacket fit for the dustbin. "Is that so? Are you looking after the children of a friend, perhaps?"

"I am their governess, sir." Though there was nothing wrong with her gloves, she tugged at them with brisk movements. "Mr. Tigg's experience is with carriages and horses. I am giving him instructions in the operation of the landau, since he aspires to be a chauffeur. Thus, he has come with us to see the engines."

Tigg, who did not even break a smile during these outrageous falsehoods, tilted his chin as if to say *See? I've as much right to be here as you.* The entrance fee had been set low on purpose, so that they were surrounded by people of all classes, from washerwomen to lords, from Wits to Bloods.

"Ah." Mr. Malvern offered her his arm. "Then may I be of use to your party? Steam locomotives, you might recall, are a particular interest of mine."

For the span of two seconds, Claire hesitated. The memory of the disdain in James Selwyn's eyes flared, and then she squelched it. Lord James was not here. Andrew Malvern, who had never shown her anything but kindness—concern, even—was.

And he could tell her and the children about engines. Perhaps he even knew something of electrick cells.

She slipped her hand into the crook of his elbow. "Thank you, Mr. Malvern, that would be most kind. Elizabeth, Margaret, Willie ... come along. This is Mr. Malvern, with the Royal Society of Engineers. He is going to tell us all about this magnificent locomotive."

Since the girls had received strict instructions that there was to be no picking of pockets, they became bored by the time the little party had walked the length of the engine. Receiving permission to go to the ice-skating rink, they ran off while Tigg, Willie, and Claire drank in every word.

"You remember the experiment I was conducting the day we met, Lady Cl—"

"Yes, I do, certainly," she said swiftly, before he used her name. "Have you had further success?"

With a sigh, he stopped, as if contemplating the row of four enormous iron wheels with their gleaming brass rods. "I wish I could say I had any success. But I cannot. I am stymied."

"Perhaps you might ask for help?"

"James isn't an engineer. He's the brains of the outfit, as they say in the Wild West, but it is I who put his ideas into motion. At the moment, however, I am making no progress at all." He looked at her sidelong from under the brim of his bowler. "What a pity you have found employment. The position is still unfilled, you know."

How could this be? "But surely any number of candidates will have jumped at it."

"Some. But having found the perfect candidate, I'm having difficulty settling for second best."

His gaze did not leave her face, and Claire's cheeks heated in a most disconcerting manner. "I—I—Mr. Tigg, what do you make of the position of the wheels under the boiler there?"

Startled, Tigg gaped at her. "Lady?"

"I mean, perhaps we might continue our tour with an exploration of electrick cells. Do you know anything of them, Mr. Malvern?"

While she pulled Willie away from his openmouthed contemplation of the engine's headlamp, set high above, she attempted to regain her composure. Goodness. Mr. Malvern could not be serious. Surely, with all the bright minds circulating in London like fireflies, he could find someone to assist him who was at least as qualified as she, if not more so? Surely he was not holding the position open in case she changed her mind?

And surely she was not even now contemplating doing so?

No, no, no. Eventually she must put those foolish dreams away. Even if she could leave the river cottage every day and drive to the laboratory, she could never tell him where she was living. And with whom. The fact was, she had painted herself into a corner with that confabulation of a story. How could a governess absent herself from her charges for hours each day? Even if she said she had left the position, there could very well be occasions when she would need to bring one or another of the children with her. There was their education to consider, after all, and what better place to conduct experiments than in a real laboratory?

Oh, no indeed. Because stories aside, what would Mr. Andrew Malvern think of a woman who made her home with cutpurses and gamblers, and who had actually slept in the rough and eaten stolen food? He would never employ such a woman if he knew that, much less ... much less hold her in esteem.

Concern.

No. He would not squander his concern on a woman with a past, nor would she ask him to. She would enjoy his company for one brief hour and never see him again.

A stout resolution, to be sure.

What a pity the thought of keeping it made her sick to her stomach.

On the other side of the Palace, their little party found an entire hall dedicated to the wonders of electrick power. "I read in the *Standard* that at night, this hall is illuminated by electricks running along channels in the ironwork structure," Andrew said. "They say it looks like a frozen lightning storm, and that you can read the paper by its light."

The young ruffian Claire had called Tigg looked doubtful. "How's that?"

Andrew pointed to the unobtrusive housings mounted next to every other support pillar, concealed by potted palms. "See those small engines there? The cells within generate the current. It's tempting to come back later, isn't it, just to see it all working."

The hint could not be any broader, but Claire only looked away. "I'm afraid the children must be at home by teatime," she said.

"Aye, some of us 'as to work," muttered Tigg.

Claire looked at him in some alarm, which seemed puzzling under the circumstances. "He means in the mews."

"Of course." Andrew could not imagine what else he might have meant.

"Mr. Malvern, perhaps we might look more closely at the small electrick cells. I am conducting a series of experiments at present and I am interested in increasing power while constraining size."

"You and every other inventor in that field." Andrew smiled, and was rewarded with a smile in return that actually reached those anxious gray eyes. "Why don't we start with the mother's helper? It's probably the most familiar to you."

"I want to see the ones on guns," Tigg said bluntly. "House things ent going to help us."

"Knowledge of firearms wouldn't help someone who plans to be a chauffeur, I wouldn't think," Andrew told him in what he hoped were quelling tones. Young upstart. If he hadn't been in Claire's company, he'd have been tempted to cuff the pup. By his age he should have learned to speak to his betters with more respect.

Tigg seemed to be swelling up with some kind of outburst, and again Claire laid a hand on his arm. "Mr. Tigg has a practical reason for his interest," she said. "And I should be glad to expand my knowledge in that area, as well. However, let us begin, as you said, with the mother's helper, and then branch off into uncharted territory once we are familiar with the basics."

Unlike similar exhibits in the British Museum, the ones in the Crystal Palace were meant to be examined and explored. The Prince Consort was keen that the technologies invented by British minds should be admired by all. Andrew was able to disassemble the mother's helper and spend an agreeable few minutes bent over it with Claire, whose own mind was so quick to grasp its principles that he suspected he was being led down the garden path.

"You've already done this, haven't you?" he finally said, as she took the loaf-shaped brass housing from his hands and snapped it into place. "You've taken one apart already and could probably tell me how it works."

"With statick repulsion," Tigg said.

"Very good, Mr. Tigg," she told him, and he straightened under her approval. Then to Andrew, she said, "I confess that I have, but my companions have not. I want Tigg and young Willie here to know as much as possible. They have ... fallen somewhat behind in their educations."

As the little boy couldn't be more than five, Andrew wondered at this, but he wouldn't contradict her for the world. "Very well, then, let us proceed to larger cells. I believe we'll find a fine example of a Winchester electrick handgun in the hall of invention for the American Territories."

Unfortunately they were not permitted to handle the Winchester piece, but a gentleman with an appalling accent and snakeskin boots was happy to show them how it worked. "This here cell replaces the old-fashioned magazine, see, where bullets used to go." He tilted it out, and Claire and Tigg craned to see the small transparent globe better. "The copper tubing runs from the cell to the barrel to protect the mechanism, see, otherwise the whole shebang would melt."

Claire's eyebrows rose. "And the copper itself does not melt?"

"No, ma'am. Copper's a conductor. So when you pull the trigger, it sets the current free, in a manner of speakin', and it travels down the barrel and out to your target."

"What's the range?" Tigg asked.

"That's a good question, pardner. Depends on the size of your cell. This here model, why, she'll zap a fly off the back of a horse from fifty feet."

Tigg's eyes widened as he contemplated this picture in his imagination, and Andrew smothered a smile.

"And what of a cell about this size?" Claire curved her hands one on top of the other, as though she were cradling a rubber ball. "What range would it have if the barrel of the piece were about three feet?"

"Ah, now you're talking rifles, which are a whole other animal. A cell that size paired with a barrel that long, why, it could take that same fly off my hypothetical horse from the end of this here exhibit hall." He pointed to the exit doors. "It's the barrel, don't you know. The bolt gets going in there and nothing can stop it. I hope you ain't planning to heft one of those, young lady. Purty little thing like you could get herself hurt."

Claire gave the Territorial a winning smile. "Of course not, sir. I'm merely seeking instruction for my young charges. Now, could I impose upon you to explain a little further how exactly the bolt is created within the cell?"

By the end of the half-hour, the American exhibitor had somehow been convinced to disassemble the Winchester and tell them about it in such detail that most people's eyes would have glazed over. But Claire Trevelyan was not most people, and neither were her companions. Andrew expected the kind of incisive questioning that Claire gave the man, but the mind of young Tigg surprised him. It was clear that a career as a chauffeur was the best he could do, considering his station—but what a waste of a fine brain. He would no doubt be the kind of driver who would while away his off days taking apart the engines and landaus of his employers and putting them back together again, just to relieve his boredom.

Claire finished her impromptu engineering class by reciting, along with Tigg, the parts that comprised the power cell, and the order in which they were assembled. From memory.

Concealing his amazement, Andrew waited as Claire thanked the gentleman for his kindness. They walked slowly down the length of the exhibit hall, stopping from time to time to examine the electrick cells on a pair of pistols, an icebox, and even on a serving trolley.

"I wonder." She halted, idly watching the trolley as it trundled from one end of a mocked-up parlor to the other.

"What's that, Lady?" Tigg's gaze followed the trolley as well.

"How big a cell do you suppose it would take to power a landau, Tigg?"

Andrew stopped himself from laughing aloud just in time. Not only would she never forgive him, but it would show disrespect in front of her students. Having been in the position of instructor before, he knew how important respect was.

"A right fair size, Lady," the boy answered. "Size of a mother's helper, for sure."

"At least." Her tone was thoughtful, as he imagined her brain turning over and over under that heap of russet hair and that ridiculous hat. Andrew wished she would share her thought processes with him, outlandish though it might be. Were they well enough acquainted that he could inquire? If only to advise her of the impossibility of such a scheme—anything bigger than household appliances had to be powered by steam. Everyone knew that.

"Hm. Yes?" She looked down as Willie tugged urgently on her skirt.

Tigg took his other hand. "Looks like 'e 'as to take a leak, Lady. Come to mention it, I do too."

This time Andrew did laugh out loud as Claire turned scarlet and clapped a hand to her mouth. "Mr. Tigg, I—really, I insist that you not—that you—oh, dear."

Andrew stepped into the breach. "Would you allow me to take them? And on the way I'll instruct them in the proper expression of such things. Shall we meet again at the ice rink to collect the girls?"

Her color still high, Claire nodded and gave him a speaking look that conveyed—what? Surely that soulful expression was more than gratitude for such a simple favor?

"Thank you. Dear me. Willie, you and Tigg are to go with Mr. Malvern, since I am superfluous in matters that concern gentlemen. I shall attempt to extricate the Mopsies from whatever disaster they have managed to create at the ice rink."

She marched away, her back straight, her skirts frothing around her ankles with the firmness of her step. What a pretty sight she was. How utterly wasted as the governess of these children. There must be some way to convince her to come and work with him.

James was around here somewhere. Andrew would prevail on him to apologize for whatever offence he had caused, and then together they would bring their powers of persuasion to bear. Now that he had found her, he would not allow her to disappear. He would have to go a long way to find a woman like this again.

As a suitable assistant.

Claire followed the direction in her guidebook and located the ice rink in only ten minutes' walk. What a miracle of technology such a simple thing was—a sheet of ice who knew how many inches thick, kept frozen by marvelous engines somewhere below. Upon it, skaters twirled on rented skates—including the Mopsies, whom she identified immediately by their shrieks of glee as they chased each other like waterbugs on blades.

It was apparent that the purchase of needle and thread on the way home would need to be followed by lessons in the homely arts of needlework. From the side of the rink Claire could see a row of lace drooping below the hems of Lizzie's dress.

Someone cleared his throat quite close to her. "It's quite a thing, isn't it, to enjoy the pleasures of January at the end of July?"

Claire's mouth went dry and instinctively she sidestepped. But there was no escaping him. Lord James Selwyn only followed. Unless she was prepared to make a scene in public, she would simply have to heap coals of fire on his head and be the soul of politeness.

"Lord James."

"Lady Claire. This is an unexpected pleasure. Though perhaps that is unfair of me. I would expect to see you in few places other than the Crystal Palace, knowing the turn of your mind."

Hmph. He knew less of the turns of her mind than Rosie the chicken, who was actually quite adept at divining what she wished to communicate. "Yes, we schoolgirls often come here to fill the gaps in our educations."

He had the grace to pause and look down at her as if he really saw her. "I take it I am not forgiven."

"That would assume you had engaged my mind enough to offend."

"You seemed very offended when last we met. Exited my laboratory with precipitous haste, if I recall."

"Your laboratory?"

"My money built it."

"Ah yes. Your money." She hoped Mrs. Morven had taken her advice about the twenty-five percent. "I trust you are satisfied with your new cook and housekeeper?"

"Mrs. Morven? That woman is a gem. A paragon. Her lemon soufflé could be presented to Her Majesty without shame."

Claire recalled the lemon soufflé with a pang of homesickness—not so much for Wilton Crescent, but for her old life and the little pleasures she had completely taken for granted.

"I'm sure you miss her sadly."

A presumptuous thing for him to say, but all too true.

"Please give her my warmest greetings and let her know I am well." It irked her to ask anything of him, but if he mentioned meeting her today, Mrs. Morven would be hurt if there were no message. She had sent a tube containing the governess story several days ago, and had received a relieved reply, along with a recipe for melted-chocolate milk—the very drink the governess used to make for Claire in the nursery long ago.

"I shall be happy to tell her," Lord James said. "May I—"

"Excuse me, Lord James. Lizzie! Maggie!" She leaned over the barrier and waved them down. "Have you enjoyed yourselves?"

"Oooh, Lady, it's the most wonderful thing, skating is," Maggie panted. "I can go backward. See?" And she wriggled—resembling nothing so much as Julia Wellesley in a new set of petticoats—and began to move in reverse, her skates carving parentheses in the ice.

Lizzie grasped her hands and together they began to move faster. "Look, Lady! Ent it grand?"

"Yes, very grand." Claire followed their progress, walking along the barricade. "But I must ask you to return to earth and hand in your skates. The others will be joining us shortly."

Reluctantly, with fits and starts and several demonstrations of skill, the girls got their skates turned in and their new patent-leather shoes buckled on. And all the while Lord James did not leave. In fact, Claire had allowed the girls' reluctance to go on far longer than she would have had he not been there, expecting his impatience to get the better of him and drive him away.

What could he be playing at, tolerating the Mopsies with such a fixed smile?

He must be up to something. And in her experience, it could not be good. She must get rid of him at once. For Andrew to find out her secrets would mean a personal loss. For Lord James to discover them would mean swift, certain, and irrevocable social disaster, to the point where she would be received by no one, not even her own mother.

"Girls, come along. We will walk this promenade and keep an eye open for Mr. Tigg and Willie."

"And who might these charming young ladies be?" Lord James's tone sounded so affable that it must be false.

The girls seemed to realize all at once that this gentleman was not just passing by, but seemed to be trying to make himself one of their party. And for a wonder, they buttoned their lips and regarded him with silent suspicion.

Snouts's training had been thorough.

"These are my charges," Claire said with admirable economy. "Margaret, Elizabeth, make your curtsies to Lord James."

Maggie turned big eyes on her sister that plainly said, *Cooooo, a real lordship,* before both girls bobbed obediently.

"Your charges?" Lord James repeated. "Do you mean to tell me you are their ... governess?"

"I am."

"And a fine one," Lizzie said without a trace of Bow's bells in her voice.

"We quite like her." Maggie took her sister's hand. "We're ever so hard on governesses."

Claire struggled not to gape, and then struggled even more with the urge to box their ears for playacting when the moment was so serious. She reached down and took Lizzie's other hand with rather more firmness than necessary.

"So nice to see you, Lord James. Good day."

"Just one moment, Lady Cl—"

"Come along, girls!"

"Wait!" he boomed just as one of those silences peculiar to large crowds fell all at once. Reddening, he collected himself. "Please, just for a moment."

If she did not listen to him, he would likely stalk her the length of the arcade. "Yes, my lord?"

He glanced to either side, but people had gone about their business. "I would have hoped for a more solicitous environment to say what I must say, but you are an elusive quarry. It seems I must take my opportunities where I find them."

"You have something you wish to say to me?" She had quite a number of things she wished to say to him, but not in front of the girls. If one wanted models of good behavior, one must be a model of good behavior oneself.

"Yes. I—well, I—" Flushing again, he chewed the lower edge of his moustache. Good heavens. He was as edgy as a man about to propose. Not that she had any experience along those lines except for what she'd seen in the flickers.

"Cat got your tongue?" Lizzie enquired.

"He's got something stuck in his throat," Maggie agreed. "Lozenge?" She held up a hard cherry drop, somewhat fuzzy from being carted about in her pocket all day.

Lord James looked down at them like Zeus from Olympus. "Little girls should be seen and not heard."

If Claire had heard that once, she'd heard it a thousand times, and every time it irritated her more. Girls should certainly be heard. It was their voices that the world was missing.

"Really, Lord James, I'll thank you to leave the girls' upbringing to me." Her tone could have been chipped right out of the sheet of ice behind them. "As it happens, I'm a great believer in little girls being heard, if they have something to say. Miss Margaret was merely offering to help."

"I was, wasn't I?" Maggie sounded very pleased.

"You're not a nice man," Lizzie told him, eyes narrowed. "You made the Lady go all frosty. You really don't want to do that."

"Great Caesar's ghost." Lord James had finally lost his patience. He glared at Claire. "You're as poor a governess as you are a scientist. All right. I'll say what I have to say, and that is this. I will offer you a thousand pounds not to take the position in Andrew's laboratory."

She could not possibly have heard him correctly. "I beg your pardon?"

"All right, then, if you will stoop to bargaining. Fifteen hundred. I know your position, my dear young lady, and that isn't the kind of sum you can turn down."

The rage came bubbling up from under her corset and into her throat. Was it possible for a man to be any more insulting?

"Isn't it?" If she said one more word, her façade would split and she would scream blue invective at him, right here, right now. The glass above their heads would crack and rain down upon him and it would serve him right for treating her in this high-handed, criminal, cruel manner.

Oh, if she were a lady in society instead of name how she would glory in crushing him to social powder under one kid heel! She would make it so that no one in their circles would receive him ever again. Even the Queen would frown when his name was mentioned. If she were—if only—

"Lady?" Maggie tugged her hand. "Look, there's Tigg and Willie with Mr. Malvern."

"Mr. Malvern?" James lifted his head like a wolf scenting the sheepdog.

Claire pulled in as deep a breath as she could, feeling her corset cinch her sides like the twin hands of caution and propriety. "Yes. He has been such a gentleman today. We've spent most of the afternoon together deepening our acquaintance and he has told us all about locomotives and steam."

Ever so sweetly, she smiled at him and allowed the girls to drag her away.

29

Like the confluence of events that results in a battle at sea, nine people converged at a single point in the cheerful arcade next to the ice-skating rink. The chamber orchestra played "Take a Pair of Sparkling Eyes" while the skaters dipped and twirled, vendors called the attention of customers to their hot meat pies and iced drinks, and Lady Julia Wellesley and Gloria Meriwether-Astor spotted Lord James and bore down upon him like two battleships under full steam.

"Lord James, how very unexpected!" Julia trilled.

"Such a pleasure to see you," Gloria added, then halted in midstep, her skirts swirling forward like foam upon the waves. "Oh, hello, Claire."

"Claire? Claire Trevelyan?" Her focus on Lord James broken, Julia looked around, her eyes registering astonishment at the number of people who had witnessed her unladylike hailing of his lordship in public. "Heavens, we thought you'd gone to Cornwall."

So much for attempting to keep her name out of the children's hearing. Well, that had been a thin hope at best.

Then Julia seemed to register Lord James's proximity to Claire, and her long lashes fluttered. "Are you ... and his lordship ... enjoying the exhibit?"

"I am, very much." Claire resented her implication that she and James were there together, and resented even more having to assure Julia that she was no threat to her pursuit. Honestly, what would it be like to live a life where such a thing was her only problem? "I cannot speak for his lordship, who was merely passing by."

Lord James had concealed all his emotion of the moment before, and had put on his public face. "Ladies, the pleasure of our meeting is all mine. Lady Julia, you look enchanting. Miss Gloria, you should build yourself a crystal palace of your own. The light of heaven suits you exactly."

Claire resisted the temptation to implore patience of that same heaven, and welcomed Andrew and the boys instead. Here was reality. No simpering exchange of insincere compliments. Instead, with them she could enjoy the meeting of like minds in pursuit of a common goal: a greater knowledge of how the world worked.

Julia and Gloria smiled and blushed. Lord James went on, "May I introduce my business partner to you?

Lady Julia Wellesley, Miss Gloria Meriwether-Astor, this is Andrew Malvern of the Royal Society of Engineers." The ladies inclined their heads while Andrew bowed.

"And what business are you working on together?" Gloria's words were polite while her eyes said, *What business does a Blood have with a Wit?*

Lord James chuckled. "I would not trouble your lovely head with it. Suffice to say we are working on making locomotive engines run more efficiently."

Lady Julia waved her hand in front of her face, as if she were overcome. "Goodness. How very droll. Do you own a railroad?"

"Not yet." He smiled at her. "But I like to engage my mind in such matters, and Andrew and I went to school together, so I knew a fine scientist who could do the practical work."

Dispensing with Andrew as unsuitable for her further attention, Lady Julia finally noticed that Claire appeared to be surrounded by children. Claire took a firm grip on the Mopsies' hands and braced herself.

"Goodness, Claire. Are all these children with you?"

"They are. Girls, make your curtsies to her ladyship. Mr. Tigg, Willie, a bow, if you please."

To her knowledge, Tigg had never bowed to anyone in his life. But having just observed Andrew, he replicated the courtesy exactly as he had seen it, and Willie imitated him so well one would think he had been born to it.

Gloria's eyebrows drew together in such a way that Claire was tempted to tell her she would have wrinkles before she was thirty if she kept it up. "Is that ... person ... with you, Claire?"

"Of course. I would not be concerned with his manners if he were not."

"I should think you'd be concerned with his clothes. Wherever did you pick him up?"

Tigg began to swell. Andrew said smoothly, "I believe Mr. Tigg is in training as a chauffeur at the children's home. Lady Claire is encouraging his interest in engines."

Both Gloria and Julia dismissed Tigg from their universe, for which Claire could only be grateful. "And who might you be?" Gloria bent as far as her corset would allow and chucked Willie under the chin. The boy tipped his head down and moved closer to Lizzie. "Don't be shy." When he still didn't respond, she straightened. "Where I come from, children speak when they are spoken to."

"Willie doesn't speak to anyone, milady," Lizzie told her. "Don't take it personal."

"Is that so. And you are?"

"Li ... Elizabeth. This is my sister Margaret."

"And how do you come to know Lady Claire, Elizabeth?"

Lizzie, don't—don't say it— Claire squeezed her hand in inarticulate warning and opened her mouth to say something—anything—

"The Lady is our governess," Lizzie said blithely. "We've been skating. Do you skate?"

Gloria did not answer. She and Julia exchanged a single incredulous look and then turned it on Claire as if they were two automatons built for a single task. "Governess?" Julia's eyebrows rose so high they practically disappeared under the flowers on her hat. *"Governess?"*

"For what family?" Gloria's voice trembled with scandalous enjoyment. "Oh, do tell, Claire, so I can send your invitation to my next ball to the correct address."

"You—you would not know them." Claire's lips felt stiff, her skin cold. Why had she chosen today to come to the exhibition? It had held nothing but humiliation and disappointment. Even her pleasure in Mr. Malvern's company had been spoiled backward by the last ten minutes.

"So they do not move in our circles?" Julia inquired.

"What I mean to say is, I am not precisely a governess." Was her voice as wretched as her blotchy scarlet face? "I am more a ... teacher. For the time being, until I find more permanent employment."

"So you are not with a family of good name and fortune?" Julia pressed. "Then these children are ... ?"

Lord, help me.

Andrew Malvern hoisted Willie up into his arms, drawing the young ladies' attention in his direction almost against their will. "As a matter of fact, I have been assisting Lady Claire in her educational efforts this very afternoon. We have a collection of fine young minds here." He smiled at her, and even in the depths of her misery, his kindness made her smile back. It was a poor effort, but his eyes twinkled when he saw it. "I have been doing my best for weeks to convince her to assist me in my laboratory, but her loyalty to her charges has thus far prevented it. I still have hope, however."

She could not bear another moment of Julia's and Gloria's smiles at her expense, however cleverly hidden behind beaded pocketbooks and gloved hands. Behind them, Lord James skewered her with his gaze. He would offer her fifteen hundred pounds to tell Andrew "no" once and for all. With it, she could return to her life and pay for a full year at the university. No one need ever know what she had been doing since that dreadful night in Wilton Crescent.

With fifteen hundred pounds, she could leave it all behind.

Willie wriggled in Andrew's arms and held his own out to her. Without thinking, she reached over and took the child, his familiar little body settling against her with the full weight of his trust.

Trust.

He had trusted her, right from the moment she had pulled herself up off the filthy road outside Aldgate Station.

What had she been thinking? She could no more betray the trust of Willie, the girls, Tigg, Jake, or Snouts than she could her own baby brother Nicholas.

No. Impossible.

Claire lifted her head and deliberately turned her shoulder to Lord James. "Mr. Malvern, you have convinced me. If we can work out a suitable arrangement for the continuing education of the children, I would be honored to assist you in your scientific efforts. Perhaps together we may yet change the landscape of the railroad industry."

His delighted astonishment was all the reward a woman could ask for.

What a pity she couldn't see the reactions behind her. Still, the silence reverberating in the air was extremely satisfying, and the brevity of their farewells even more so.

As she and her little party walked slowly toward the exit, the light playing over them as though even Heaven approved of her boldness, Claire couldn't help the flutter of nerves in her stomach. Once again, she had burned a bridge behind her—this time, for all the best reasons.

Only time would tell if she had done the right thing.

She lifted her face to the sky as, surrounded by her accidental family, she stepped out of the mighty glass doors and into her future.

Epilogue

My dear Claire,

I am this very morning in receipt of a tube from my aunts Beaton, who say they have not seen you at all these past three weeks. I confess your behavior puzzles and distresses me. You were to have concluded the affairs of our move and joined me here in Cornwall. Instead, you have embarked on a mad scheme to find employment. It is enough that I must contemplate the thought of my daughter earning her bread in such a thankless manner. But to know so little of how or why—I cannot bear it.

What is the name of the family in whose bosom you have found such employment? Are they socially accept-

able? If you must do this, I would expect nothing less than the children of a duke, dear. I would also expect you would keep your situation utterly unknown to our acquaintance. Find some way of swearing the duke and duchess to secrecy. I insist upon it.

Dear Heaven, Claire, you make it increasingly difficult for me to find you a suitable husband. How can you be so headstrong when my faculties are barely adequate to see to the tasks I have at hand?

Have you heard from Mr. Arundel? I find I am out of pocket far sooner than I expected. He must find a way to locate what your father used to call working capital, otherwise, I shall be forced to let some of the staff go.

Inform me at once of your situation. If I do not find it suitable, I shall contact Gorse and prevail upon him to bring you down to Cornwall by main force if necessary.

Ever your loving
Mother

THE END

A Note from Shelley

Dear reader,

I hope you enjoy reading the adventures of Lady Claire and the gang in the Magnificent Devices world as much as I enjoy writing them. It is your support and enthusiasm that is like the steam in an airship's boiler, keeping the entire enterprise afloat and ready for the next adventure.

You might leave a review on your favorite retailer's site to tell others about the books. And you can find the print editions of the entire series online.

Do visit me on my website at www.shelleyadina.com, which includes Claire's personal correspondence in the "Letters from the Lady" series on my blog. I invite you to sign up for my newsletter there, too.

And now, for an excerpt from the next book in the series, I invite you to turn the page ...

HER OWN DEVICES
BY SHELLEY ADINA
© 2011

HER OWN DEVICES

1

London, August 1889

They were too small to be airships, and too ephemeral to be bombs. Glowing with a gentle orange light, each the size of a lantern, they floated up into the night sky powered by a single candle and the most delicate of tiny engines.

One didn't, after all, simply release such dangerous things without a means of directing where they were to go.

"They're so pretty," Maggie breathed.

"Sh!" Her twin sister Lizzie, both of them having no surname that anyone knew, nudged her with urgency. "The Lady said to be quiet."

SHELLEY ADINA

"You be quiet! Since when d'you listen to the Lady at the best o' times?"

"Mopsies!" Lady Claire Trevelyan, sister of a viscount, formerly a resident of Belgravia and now a resident of a hideout in Vauxhall gained at the price of a brigand's life, glared at both girls. They'd been on many a night lookout. What were they thinking, to risk giving away their position by whispering?

Though Claire had to admit that the beauty of the balloons' dreamy flight hid the fact that she, Jake, and Tigg had constructed them out of a rag picker's findings: a silk chemise, a ragged nightgown so fine she could draw it through her grandmother's emerald ring, a pair of bloomers that a very broad lady had thrown away because of a tear she was too wealthy to mend.

Add to this a little device Claire had been working on that would act as a steering and propulsion mechanism, and you had a set of silent intruders that could go where she and her accomplices could not.

Hunching their shoulders at the reproof, the girls settled behind the tumbledown remains of a churchyard wall to watch the half-dozen balloons sail away with their cargo over the width of a street and up over a two-story stone wall as impregnable as a medieval keep.

The spider takes hold with her hands, and is in kings' palaces. Well, tonight she was the spider and the inhabitants of "The Cudgel" Bonaventure's fortress were about to learn a lesson in manners. One did not jump the associates of the Lady in the street and relieve them of the rewards of their night's work in the gambling parlors without reprisal. The candles that caused the balloons to rise would not set his fortress on fire, but the chemical suspended in a single vial from each certainly would.

An owl hooted, rather more cheerfully than one might expect. "They're over the wall," Snouts McTavish translated. "We can move in when you give the word, Lady."

"I think it will be safe to wait for Mr. Bonaventure in the street. Jake, do you have the gaseous capsaicin devices should he prove foolish?"

"Aye."

She had known Jake for several weeks. Even now, she was not sure he wouldn't use such a device on her and challenge Snouts for lieutenancy of their little band of the abandoned and neglected. However, if someone were to prove himself trustworthy, he must perforce be trusted. Leaving him in charge of the satchel with its clinking contents was a calculated risk, but it was one she must take. Especially since he had compounded the devices himself.

"Right, then. Let us offer advice to the distressed and homeless, shall we?"

The glow over the wall was bright enough to light their way into the street as the buildings behind it caught fire. The contents of each vial suspended beneath its balloon had ignited on contact with air as the candles burned out and they dropped out of flight, higgledy-piggledy all over the roof of The Cudgel's headquarters. Wood that had been dried out during the hot summer—old wood, that had been standing

since long before their glorious Queen's time—ignited
and in seconds the oldest part of the building had gone
up like a Roman candle.

Claire regretted the loss of the steering mechanisms—a particularly nice bit of engineering she was
quite proud of—but at least they had gone in a good
cause.

The Cudgel would think twice before picking on her
friends again.

The entire house was engulfed in roaring flame by
the time the single gate creaked open and a small
crowd of men and boys tumbled through it, gasping
and slapping smoldering sparks and holding bits of
clothing over their faces against the smoke.

Hmph. And where were the women holding positions in The Cudgel's hierarchy? Her opinion of his
leadership dropped even lower.

The wailing of the fire engines in the distance told
her she must be succinct.

"Mr. Bonaventure!" she called, stepping into full
view in the middle of the street. She had dressed carefully in raiding rig for the occasion, in a practical black
skirt that could be rucked up by means of internal
tapes should she have to run or climb. She had dis-
pensed with a hat for the evening, choosing instead to
simply leave her driving goggles sitting in front of her
piled hair, a gauzy scarf wound over it and around her
neck. A leather corselet contained a number of hooks
and clasps for equipment, and instead of her trusty
rucksack, which Jake was wearing, she now wore a
leather harness with a spine holster specially made to

the contours of the lightning rifle she had taken from Lightning Luke Jackson three weeks ago. She was pleased to see that her lacy blouse remained pristine white, despite the half-hour spent huddled behind the wall.

She slid the rifle from its holster over her shoulder and held it loosely, her index finger hovering over the power switch.

In ones and twos, the small crowd of smoked criminals realized what she held—and therefore, who she was. Slowly, they backed against the wall, leaving The Cudgel exposed to her aim.

Hmph. So much for honor among thieves.

The Cudgel eyed her. "I know you. Wot business you got 'ere?"

The sirens sounded closer. They would be crossing the Southwark Bridge over the Thames even now. "Just this," she said, enunciating crisply so that there would be no misunderstanding. "Last night your men set upon four of my friends returning from the gaming halls, and took everything they had. This is a warning to you that I do not tolerate abuse of my friends or the fruit of their honest labor."

"Izzat so," he drawled. "Can't say as I know wot yer babbling on."

She hefted the rifle and pushed the power switch. "I suggest you apply your limited intellect to it."

His head thrust forward like that of an angry bull-dog whose bone has just been ripped from its teeth. "I say you go back to your needlepoint like a good little girl and think about wot I'm goin' to do to you for—"

The gun hummed happily, its pitch and frequency announcing that it was ready for work. Claire's index finger now rested on the trigger.

"If I hear that you have stepped foot in Vauxhall, with or without evil intent, your own yellow belly will be the last thing you ever see."

Yellow belly? Goodness. That was a line straight out of one of the melodramatic flickers she and Emilie had been addicted to centuries ago—two months ago—when she had been a green girl.

"I'd say you owe me, then, girlie—"

"You may address me as the Lady."

He started across the street. "And you must address *this*. Creeper! Hiram! Hold her down." He fumbled with the buttons on his trousers, while Claire stared in astonishment. Really. With the fire engines nearly upon them and his house burning to cinders as they spoke, he thought he could threaten her by means of his disgusting person?

Creeper and Hiram, whoever they were, did not, in fact, hold her down. However, two shadows detached from the main body of the huddle and slipped away down the alley at the corner of the wall. Snouts, Jake, and Tigg formed an immovable mass at her back.

Claire sighed. "Really, Mr. Bonaventure. You should not, as my mother often told me, use a pin when a needle is called for. Particularly so dull and short a pin."

She pulled the trigger and a bolt of lightning shot across the street, singeing him neatly between the legs and burning the inner seams of his canvas trousers clean away.

The Cudgel screamed and leaped back six feet, the scent of burning flesh overlaid on the smoke that filled the air. Hysterical, no doubt in pain at least equal to that he had hoped to inflict upon her, he capered and screeched so that Claire could hardly distinguish between him and the sirens of the engines as they roared up the cobbled street.

"Billy Bolt!" With the signal to scatter, her friends slipped into the shadows with her before anyone in authority could say they'd been there.

Snouts waited until they were nearly back in their own neighborhood before he said, "Been gettin' a little target practice in, I see. It'll look like 'e got burnt by the fire and none o' that lot will say different."

"I have indeed." The furthest corner of the garden wall was scorched and pockmarked as proof. "There is no point in being considered armed and dangerous if one cannot actually hit anything."

"Lucky that gun is accurate."

"It's more than accurate, Snouts. You've seen yourself how it practically *feels* your aim. Even Willie could hit a target with it, I'm sure."

"Lady, please tell me you ent gonna—"

"No, certainly not. No one touches this rifle but me ... or you, when you are acting in my stead. It's more than just a weapon, you know. It stands for what we've accomplished."

Snouts said no more, just kept pace with her, one eye on the others to make sure no one fell behind and no one was in pursuit, and the other on the street ahead, watching for danger.

Claire was the first to admit that keeping order in a band of thieves and cutpurses would be nearly impossible without the rifle—or rather, without their belief in what she might do with it. The truth was, she had only fired it outside the garden three times: Twice on the night it had come into her possession, and tonight.

Clearly she had inherited not only her father's aptitude for firearms, but also his belief that one did not need to speak much, only to say what was worth hearing when one did. Or, as Polgarth the poultryman at the family pile in Cornwall was wont to say, *Walk soft an' carry a big stick.*

She was thankful that at least Snouts, Tigg, and the Mopsies followed her lead without coercion. Since she had lost her home in the Arabian Bubble riots and fallen in with this street gang that was no more than a rabble of desperate, hungry children, they had taught her how to survive—and she had taught them how to thrive.

Between lessons in reading and mathematics, they rehearsed new and confounding hands of Cowboy Poker, the current rage they had fabricated in the drawing rooms and gambling halls of London. Those with a bent for chemistry and mechanics assisted her in the assembly of her devices. Food appeared on the table with heartening regularity now, and they all had more than one suit of clothes each. Even Rosie, the hen she had rescued, who ruled the desolate garden behind the cottage with an iron claw, had begun to put on weight.

And to top it all, tomorrow she was to begin employment as assistant to Andrew Malvern, M.Sc., Royal Society of Engineers.

The watchman on the roof platform above the river entrance whistled, and Snouts whistled three notes in return. The door swung open, allowing a wide bar of warm light to spill onto the planks that had been repaired after a series of unfortunate explosions caused by the previous inhabitants.

"Lady! You're back. What happened?" Lewis asked eagerly before he was fairly through the door.

Weepin' Willie, a mute boy of five, pushed through the legs of the boys crowding the porch, and flung himself into Claire's arms. She hugged him, a warm rush of gratitude spilling through her that here, at least, was one person in all the world who loved her without reservation. The others respected her, perhaps even liked her. But this small scrap of humanity had stuck to her like a burr from the moment she'd met him. Because of him—well, because of them all, really, she'd kept to her course and not gone down to Cornwall beaten and defeated, to be the bride of some country squire chosen by her mother.

"The Cudgel will not be waylaying any of you in the future," she told them, setting Willie on his feet and getting up. "He has a permanent reminder to mind his manners henceforth."

Snouts made a gesture in the vicinity of his pants that caused the boys' eyes to widen in horror and admiration.

She was committed to her new life now, for good or ill.

Of course, The Cudgel aside, avoiding ill was at the top of her list of priorities. For that reason, she had allowed her new employer to believe she was the governess of five of these children, and part of their agreement was that they might supplement their education in his laboratory on occasion.

Surely she would be able to keep her secret. After all, he had not inquired too closely about her place of residence or who, exactly, would allow their children out with her to perform experiments in a riverside warehouse. She would just have to remain pleasantly vague about certain details, and trust that his natural reserve and politeness would prevail.

It would never do for him to know that he was harboring the infamous Lady of Devices, inadvertent murderer of Lightning Luke Jackson and reigning queen of the south side underworld.

Her reputation in society would never recover.

About the Author

The official version

RITA Award® winning author and Christy finalist Shelley Adina wrote her first novel when she was 13. It was rejected by the literary publisher to whom she sent it, but he did say she knew how to tell a story. That was enough to keep her going through the rest of her adolescence, a career, a move to another country, a B.A. in Literature, an M.F.A. in Writing Popular Fiction, and countless manuscript pages.

Shelley is a world traveler who loves to imagine what might have been. Between books, she loves playing the piano and Celtic harp, making period costumes, and spoiling her flock of rescued chickens.

The unofficial version

I like Edwardian cutwork blouses and velvet and old quilts. I like bustle drapery and waltzes and new sheet music and the OED. I like steam billowing out from the wheels of a locomotive and autumn colors and chickens. I like flower crowns and little beaded purses and jeweled hatpins. Small birds delight me and Roman ruins awe me. I like old books and comic books and new technology ... and new books and shelves and old technology. I'm feminine and literary and practical, but if there's a beach, I'm going to comb it. I listen to shells and talk to hens and ignore the phone. I believe in thank-you notes and kindness, in commas and friendship, and in dreaming big dreams. You write your own life. Go on. Pick up a pen.

AVAILABLE NOW

The Magnificent Devices series:
Lady of Devices
Her Own Devices
Magnificent Devices
Brilliant Devices
A Lady of Resources

Caught You Looking (contemporary romance, Moon-shell Bay #1)
Immortal Faith (paranormal YA)
Peep, the Hundred-Decibel Hummer (early reader)
The All About Us series of six books
(contemporary YA, 2008–2010)

To learn about my Amish women's fiction written as Adina Senft, visit www.adinasenft.com.
The Wounded Heart
The Hidden Life
The Tempted Soul
And in 2014, the Healing Grace series beginning with
Herb of Grace

SHELLEY ADINA

COMING SOON

CPSIA information can be obtained at www.ICGtesting.com
Printed in the USA
LVOW07s1755040615

441210LV00006B/761/P

9 781463 549992